# MY FAIR APPRENTICE

## By
## Rose Lyley

# Triskelion Publishing

## www.triskelionpublishing.net

*All about women. All about extraordinary.*

"This was a fabulous story! I was enthralled the minute I started it and couldn't put it down. With vivid descriptions, engaging characters and an intriguing storyline storytelling magic as she tells the tale of Alasdair and Meg. Alasdair is a delicious hero and Meg is spunky, witty and perfectly loveable. Full of passion, humor and surprising twists, this story will quickly become a favorite."

*Susan Biliter, **eCataRomance Reviews***

"The tension between Meg and Alasdair simmers with passion. Alasdair is a hot and sensual male. You will definitely want to read this story again and again."

*Jennifer Brooks, **Coffee Time Romance***

"The characters in this novel are three-dimensional, even the secondary and bit players. The hero, Mac, and the heroine, Meg, are extremely complex people, which comes across in the writing. I enjoyed seeing Mac and Meg's relationship grow and deepen throughout the book.

The supporting plot had just enough suspense, and a lot of love scenes. I thought the love scenes themselves were emotional and fulfilling, and hovered just between sensuous and erotic – the love scenes were detailed and yet the author refrained from using the graphic wording which can be offensive to some readers. I liked this book a lot – in fact, it's a keeper!"

*Jean, **Fallen Angel Reviews***

Published by Triskelion Publishing
15327 W. Becker Lane
Surprise, AZ 85379
U.S.A.

Originally e-published by Triskelion Publishing as Tempting Fate by Esther Mitchell

Printing history:
First e-published by Triskelion Publishing
First e-publishing January 2005
First paperback printing June 2006

ISBN 1-933874-05-8

## CHAPTER ONE

Bored, bored, bored. Great Stars, he was bored out of his mind! With a disgusted sigh, Alasdair MacCorran leaned back into the darkened corner of the coffee shop booth and watched the snow outside drifting lazily toward the ground, where people in far too much hurry to do absolutely nothing important would trample it. He knew how that felt. Not the trampling part– no one in their right mind would even attempt to run over a MacCorran– but the having nothing important to do. He'd become jaded to it all.

His eyes traveled the interior of the coffee shop, and he suppressed another sigh. *Hole in the Wall*, whimsically named by its original owner for the since-patched holes in the brick exterior, was a small, secluded hangout for Seattle's more offbeat crowd. The last place anyone would ever expect to find Alasdair MacCorran, Master *Draoidh* of the *Sgàil Ealdhainean* and descendant of the *Cheud Draoidh* of the *Sgàil Taighean*. Not that he gave a damn, he decided with a disdainful snort, for the world he'd left behind. Come to think of it, he didn't care about anything in three dimensions, anymore, not even his magic. That thought had troubled him for a while. Magic had always thrilled him, the rush of power in his veins too seductive to resist. So, why did it suddenly bore him? What was missing? Why did he keep feeling like something important was lacking?

"Mac? Hela's teats, man, snap out of it!"

Roused from his musings, Mac quirked a dark brow at his companion. They were probably as different as any two friends could be, he and Geoff. Mac bore all the hereditary traits of his Celtic ancestors – he had their wiry, athletic build, skin of a smooth olive tone, hair darker than midnight, and eyes that were a pure, deep bronze. Geoff Grayson – Geoffrey Grayson IV, Master *Skald* of the *Thorolfkin*, to be proper – was Norse from the roots of his moon-blond hair to the toes of his fur-lined biker boots, a giant who appeared at once intimidating and approachable. Mac was the dark side of their duo, and always had been, ever since they'd suffered through Madame Luminare's Elementary Magic at the age of six. Geoff was the very definition of laid-back observer, half-lost in his stories. Now, though, he sounded more like the *Thorolfkind* – the dark wolf – he really was. He was miffed about something.

"What was that?" Mac enquired blandly, leaning back in the booth and twisting a strand of shadow around his finger, pulling it around to mask his face.

Geoff shoved a large hand through his long, blond hair in a frustrated gesture, his sharp, canine teeth flashing in the light as he grated out, "I swear by all the Gods, Mac, you're getting senile, living out there in the woods! I asked if you're ready for *Luna Ascesa*, yet."

Ready? Mac bit out a sharp laugh. *Luna Ascesa*, or Rising Moon, was the biggest gala and trade conference in the magic world, and each master of a field had to choose one apprentice under them to represent their Craft with a display of skills. As Master of the *Sgàil Ealdhainean* – the realm of shadow magics– Mac should have a dozen or more apprentices to choose from. Only, he'd grown bored with apprentices, and teaching, years ago. He'd dismissed his last pupil after *Luna Ascesa* last year. Hellfire, he was bored with magic!

"I'm not going."

Geoff, in the process of taking a drink of his coffee, nearly spit the contents of his mug across the booth. Choking, he finally spluttered, "What do you mean, you're not going? You don't have a *choice*, Mac! None of us do."

Mac shrugged indifferently. "I've been banned, by now."

Geoff sat back, frowning. "How's that?"

Gods and demons, shape-shifters could be thick, at times! Mac rolled his eyes expressively. "Because I broke taboo."

Understanding dawned in Geoff's keen azure eyes. "Ah. The infamous female apprentice." He leaned forward, resting his arms on the table as his eyes sparkled with interest. "I've been wondering about that one, myself. You knew it was taboo for a man to teach a woman – we have different arts and different training techniques where the arts overlap – so why'd you thumb your nose at tradition? You're not a rebel, Mac."

Mac sighed, leaning further into the shadows, wishing he could just make himself disappear into them. He could, of course, but it wouldn't get him out of this. Geoff already knew that juvenile trick. Finally, he faced his friend. "You're telling me you haven't found it odd that, since I took on this apprentice, you've never seen her?"

Geoff's frown deepened. "There is that. Who is she?"

Mac bit out a sharp laugh. "I have no idea."

"*Excuse* me?" Geoff blinked, hard. "You've been living with and mentoring this woman for almost a year, and—"

"Geoff," Mac leaned forward suddenly, and saw surprise flicker through his friend's eyes. Shadow magic tended to have that effect, even on magic users. "That's the whole damned point! There *is* no woman."

There was silence from the other side of the table for a full minute before Geoff loosed a low, disbelieving groan and slumped back in his seat. "I'm not hearing this! Mac, please tell me you didn't deliberately falsify yourself to the *Illuminata*."

Mac nodded glumly, sinking back into the shadows again. "It gets worse."

"I don't want to know how, buddy."

"Tough," Mac returned in dark humor. "You asked. I'm sick of magic, Geoff. There's no thrill, no challenge, anymore. I can create or conjure anything I want with a wave of my hand." He demonstrated, sugar and cream poured out of thin air into his coffee.

"Uh, Mac," Geoff said hesitantly. "You

drink your coffee black, man."

Mac waved his hand and the coffee returned to the dark, inky brew it'd been before. "That's not the point."

"Okay, so you've hit a slump," the blond giant said with a shrug. "We all do at some point. What's that got to do with lying to the *Illuminata*? Man, they can take away *everything* for that!"

Mac snorted disdainfully, spreading his hands wide in indifference. "They can have it all, if they want it. I don't care anymore."

"That's it," Geoff muttered with shake of his blond head. "You've officially run mad from all that communing with nature. Mac, you know as well as I do what happens if they find out you lied. You'll lose it all. Not just the money, or the license to practice magic in this dimension, man, but *everything*! They'll give you the Mark of the Damned, man. You'll be stripped of your magic, and you'll disgrace the MacCorrans forever. What about your parents? What about Ysabet, Mac?"

Mac straightened, his bronze eyes blazing. "Leave Ys out of this."

Geoff snorted derisively. "I didn't bring her into it, *you* did, you dumb bastard. The *Illuminata* find out you lied about an apprentice, and Ysabet won't have a snowball's chance in Hell of ever getting into a Bardic school, no matter *who* sponsors her."

Mac groaned, slumping back into the comforting embrace of the shadows. Geoff was right! He'd been a self-centered ass to submit

that false résumé.  Ysabet was barely sixteen –
their parents' late-life surprise and joy – and the
only thing that still shed any light in Mac's dark
existence.  He couldn't let his sister pay for his
stupidity!

"What am I going to do?  *Luna Ascesa* is
only a little over a month away, Geoff."

Geoff shrugged nonchalantly.  "Hey, it's
your mess, Mac.  But I'd suggest you find
someone, and quick.  You've got a lot of work to
do in a month."

Mac snorted.  "You know the *Sgàil
Ealdhainean* are way too complicated for just
anyone to learn."

"But I'll bet you can do it.  If there's anyone
pigheaded enough to turn a nobody into a *Sgàil
Ealdhainean Bhuitseach*, it's you."

Mac rolled his eyes.  "Fat lot of help you
are."

"Fine."  Geoff leaned forward, suddenly all
hunter.  "How about a little wager, MacCorran?
You get off your ass and use all that charm and
magic you ooze all over the place to turn the
next woman who passes this table into
everything you put in that résumé, and I'll
personally browbeat Kyna Ravensfall into
slating your sister for the next entry sitting at
Dalamor."

Mac's brows shot up as his eyes widened.
Ysabet would give her right eye to get into
Dalamor Bardic Academy.  It was the most
prestigious Bardic school in three dimensions,
and entry sittings were impossible to get
without the approval of the highly critical

Headmistress. Ysabet would be ecstatic, and really, how hard could it be to train a woman in the *Sgàil Ealdhainean*? *Hole in the Wall* was a meeting place for Seattle's Pagan types. Surely, he could train one of this dimension's *Draoi*, or even a Wiccan, with a minimal amount of fuss. It was an easy win. A slow, confident smirk sliding over his face, Mac met his friend's challenging gaze.

"You're on, Grayson."

Geoff looked up, and grinned wolfishly. "Good. Don't look now, my friend, but your subject's headed our way."

Mac blinked and looked around, but there was no one there. No one except a harried-looking and unkempt waitress, her dark hair working loose from her braid in flyaway strands of curly frizz.

"Where? I don't see anyone."

Geoff tipped his head back and laughed as the waitress passed their table, scowling. "You now have an official apprentice, Mac. You just saw her."

Mac's eyes landed on the waitress, and horror settled. "Not her."

"Remember the bet, Mac. The next woman to pass our table." Geoff gave the waitress an once-over, his eyes twinkling. "Well, she's female, and she walked right past us. Looks like she's your girl, buddy."

His eyes fixed on the woman's stormy scowl and flyaway hair, Mac bit back a disbelieving groan. He'd heard of turning sow's ears into silk purses before but this was ridiculous.  He was going to lose this bet, big time.

## CHAPTER TWO

That did it, it was official. The Universe at large was out to get her. Meg Tempest slapped her damp cleaning rag down on the sticky surface of the window table where someone's kid had smeared honey handprints. This was supposed to be her day off. And not just any day off, this was supposed to be the day her life changed, and she got out of the massive disaster it had been for twenty-eight years. She'd had it all set up, at last. She was supposed to audition with the Seattle Philharmonic Orchestra, for the chance to sit as their new pianist, in exactly three minutes. Yet, here she was, cleaning up someone else's messes and missing her dream, all because whatever god there was up there was one sick practical joker.

"Murphy's Law," she muttered to herself, shaking her head at the phrase her mother had used one too many times in her life, to explain all the mishaps she suffered. "I'll show you Murphy's Law. If I ever find Murphy, he's a dead man!"

A throat cleared, somewhere near her, startling Meg. She turned from her furious scrubbing, and felt the air stop in her lungs. God. She hoped this was Murphy, because she could handle a little drawn-out revenge. Beside her stood the most gorgeous specimen of male beauty she'd ever laid eyes on.

He was probably six-foot-two or three, towering over her five-foot-six and a half inches and making her feel positively diminutive. His olive complexion was deeper than her skin tone with eyes that gleamed like pennies in the dim lighting of the coffee house. Molasses-brown hair curled against his collar, looking so thick and silky her fingers itched to run through it.

She licked her lips, and saw something dark and dangerous flash in his eyes, before wry humor curled on his lips. Her heart pounded so loudly she was sure he could hear it, and her skin tingled with the touch of his eyes as they skimmed over her. Did he find her reaction funny? Defensive fury roused in her, and she lifted her chin belligerently and said, "Seen enough? Maybe you can tell me what you want, now?"

An ebony brow quirked, but Meg refused to back down from the humor that flashed there. He'd be laughing out of the other end once she got through with him, boy-toy material or not.

He must have read her intention in her face, because he suddenly chuckled, and the deep, mysterious sound quaked along her tautly strung nerve endings, sending heat lightning ricocheting through Meg. She shivered at the wave of heat, and barely controlled a small moan. She wasn't going to let a stranger see that he affected her at all.

Especially not this one.

He had dangerous written all over him. From his severely handsome, exotic features to his tight black jeans and gray silk shirt, he was the stuff dark fantasies were made of. In fact, he'd probably feature in one or two of hers, in coming months. Yet, there was something else about him – a shadowy self-confidence, a powerful presence – that made her insides melt at the thought of what kind of lover he'd make. Fantasy material, for sure.

"When you're finished…"

His husky brogue rolled over her, taking Meg's breath away. It took her a moment to register what he'd actually said. When she did, she blinked hard.

"Finished what?"

He chuckled again, his eyes sparkling with mirth. "Stripping me with your eyes."

Of all the arrogant, conceited…  "I was not."

He leaned closer, until she felt surrounded by him, his scent all around her, as dark and mysterious as a shadow, and so utterly perfect her heart nearly stopped.

"No sense lying to me, lass. Your eyes give you away." He reached out and tilted her chin up until she was forced to meet his bronze gaze. A spark kindled there, and he seemed almost surprised. "Such lovely eyes they are. Like sweet, dark honey…"

Meg swallowed hard, and yanked her face from his light grasp. She felt too raw, too exposed, under that piercing gaze of his. She could feel her hackles rising, and welcomed the return of her control.

"What do you want?" She snapped as she went back to her task.

"Your name."

"Can't have it," she replied flippantly. "I already own it, and it's not for sale."

His hand moved to her hair, and she felt the light tug as he wrapped one dark, unruly strand around his index finger. "Sarcasm, my pet, doesn't become you."

"At the moment, it's the only thing standing between you and a mouth full of broken teeth, so don't knock it, buster." Meg scrubbed harder. His *pet*? How obnoxious could a man possibly get? This one might be sexy as hell, but it was no wonder the man was still single. A glance at his left hand confirmed that. He'd drive any woman crazy inside of a day, with that attitude. "And I'm not your *anything*."

A brief smile flickered at his lips as she shot him a glare. "Have it your way, *leannan*. I'll learn your name soon enough."

Her eyes narrowed at the smug confidence in his smirk. He was arrogant, and yet, there was a steely determination to his eyes that told her he spoke only the truth. She sighed resignedly. *Might as well get it over with, now.* She slapped the rag down on the table and turned to face him, planting her fists on her hips as she glared up at him. "Meg, okay? My name's Meg. Now, leave me alone, or tell me what you want. I'm busy."

He reached to remove one fist from her hip never knowing how close he was to a quick, painful death, and raised it to his lips in a smooth European fashion she imagined melted other women. Not her. Well, okay, maybe her knees trembled a little as his warm, firm lips brushed her skin, but that was because she hadn't had any in so long she was probably an honorary virgin, again. It had nothing to do with *him*.

Swallowing hard at the sudden image of how she could end her dry spell with this man, she snatched her hand away. The images were just too tempting, and she couldn't afford the distraction. "Who are you?"

"Alasdair MacCorran, Laird of Lachulan Castle, among other things." He quirked a smile full of wry, self-mocking humor, and Meg nearly groaned in disbelief. Oh, great. Another escapee from the loony bin, trying to get her attention. How did she always end up with these morons?

"I see."

A small frown furrowed his brow, just above those sensual eyes, as he studied her. Then, his brow smoothed, and he smiled. "I doubt you do. However, I do have a proposition for you."

Those words stabbed Meg with surprise, before angry heat fanned her face. Did she *look* that easy?

"Okay, that's my cue. This conversation is over, Mr. MacCorran, or whoever the hell you really are." She snatched up her rag and turned away, before she hauled off and socked a customer. Phil the Pill wouldn't like that.

"Wait!" His hand closed around her arm, causing Meg to spin around in automatic defense. "Just listen—"

"No." She shook off his grip on her arm, her eyes stormy. She'd had enough. This had been the day from hell already, and she'd had to sacrifice her dreams, once again. She wasn't about to listen to any crackpot. "You listen to me. I'm sick and tired of being pestered by men like you, who think the only way to get to know a woman is to flatter her with a bunch of syrupy endearments and crawl inside her panties. Newsflash, buster: I don't want you, I don't plan on sleeping with you, *or* with your friend over there, and I certainly don't need your kind of trouble in my life. So just take your noble ass back over to your booth and—"

"Miss Tempest!" A nasal, grating voice screeched from behind her making Meg wince. Great. Phil the Pill, owner of *Hole in the Wall*, finally puts in an appearance and, of course, it would be just in time to hear her tell a rude customer off. "What do you think you're doing?"

"Nothing," she muttered, glaring up into Alasdair MacCorran's wry grin.

"Well, you can take your nothing right out that door and down the street to the unemployment office," Phil huffed, puffing up like an overstuffed penguin. "You're fired."

Mac watched the look of stunned disbelief that crossed Meg Tempest's intriguing honey-brown eyes, and wondered whether she was more surprised she'd been fired so easily and publicly, or that she'd let her temper get the best of her like she had. Then, as fury whipped to life in her eyes again, Mac decided it must be the former.  He sighed in resignation, wondering if his friend had set him up once again.  There was no way he could teach this woman the complexities of the *Sgàil Ealdhainean* in a month, he'd be lucky if he could teach her to control that storm brewing in her eyes.

Without a word, Meg whipped off the apron around her waist and threw it straight into the face of the pompous little ass who'd fired her, and then, shooting Mac a glare that told him she reserved the top slot of her shit list for him alone, stormed toward the front door. But, rather than the fury he supposed he should rightly be terrified of, it was the flicker of raw vulnerability that had crossed her eyes that intrigued Mac.  And, just as he saw her figure disappearing down the snowy Seattle street, there was a hiss and a pop, and the entire interior of the coffee shop plunged into darkness.

## CHAPTER THREE

"Damn it!" The short, balding proprietor of *Hole In the Wall* was behind the coffee shop's wide counter before Mac could blink, getting in another waitress' face. Mac winced at the other man's shrill, nasal tone. It was enough to annoy the dead to rising, even from across the small building. He felt instant pity for the young woman on the receiving end of that up-close verbal assault. "What's happened *now*?"

"S-sorry, Mr. Blackman," the pale-faced girl behind the counter was practically shaking in the dim light that filtered in from the street. "The new espresso machine just... it just blew up! I guess it just blew a fuse, or something."

"It's that damned Tempest woman, again!" Blackman seethed, heedless of the busy shop as he slapped the counter with one hand. "That woman's a menace!"

Mac's brows shot up and his eyes flew to the door Meg Tempest had stormed out as Blackman's words rang in his ears. *Again?* Did that mean Meg, of the sharp tongue and gorgeous eyes, had been responsible for more than one disaster around here? Mac frowned. She didn't seem the type to deliberately sabotage anything, but it was either that, or she had to have the world's worst luck. Mac closed his eyes and suppressed a groan. No way. He didn't want to teach a woman whom disaster followed around.

"This is getting better by the minute."

Mac started and turned at the sound of his friend's voice. He'd nearly forgotten Geoff was there, or that his friend had got him into this mess in the first place. He'd been too busy getting lost in a pair of honey-brown eyes, and a wit that was as enchanting as it was contrary. Mac shifted as his interest stirred in a way that was anything but helpful. Meg Tempest was far too fascinating for comfort.

"This isn't going to work," he muttered with a shake of his head.

"What are you, now? A Doomsayer?" Geoff scoffed. "C'mon. She's got to be the perfect candidate for apprenticeship! She blacked out the whole building, Mac." The big man gave him a hardy slap on the shoulder. "I bet even you would be hard-pressed to go that far!"

"You might want to watch that tendency to make bets," Mac returned dryly. "It'll get you, and me, into trouble."

Geoff scowled. "Quit stalling, Mac. You couldn't ask for better apprentice material than that woman!"

"If I had a decade to spend teaching her, maybe," Mac hedged doubtfully, his concerned eyes trained on the gusting snow outside. He wondered where Meg had gone. Hopefully somewhere warm, she hadn't grabbed a coat or anything before she disappeared out the door. That concern startled him. Since when did he care what anyone did? It was the bet, he told himself. He felt responsible, after approaching her the way he had. Her reaction flashed through him, and he winced. "Geoff, she can't even control her temper. How's a woman like that going to learn how to control volatile magic like the *Sgàil Ealdhainean*?"

Geoff shrugged, and chuckled. "You'll find a way, Mac. You always do."

Not this time. Mac stifled the uneasy feeling his world was about to be upended without his permission. It was a feeling he hated. With a glance at his friend, he sighed. "You're serious about this."

A strange, somber light flared in Geoff's keen, lupine eyes. "Never more. A bet's a bet, MacCorran."

Mac's eyes narrowed. Whatever he might claim, Geoff had a very personal reason to hold him to this insane bet. Mac could see it, he read it in the shadows that crossed his friend's face. With another sigh – this one of resignation – Mac grabbed his leather jacket on his way toward the door. What he'd let himself in for this time, he didn't know, but if the tightening knot in his stomach was any indication, it was trouble. Whatever it turned out to be, he knew boredom, at very least, was about to become a thing of the past.

*****

Following Meg was child's play for a man of his abilities. The shadow imprints of her passage glowed like flaming beacons on the astral plane, stronger than any being of this realm he'd ever encountered. Dear Gods of

Shadow, it was amazing she hadn't yet been
discovered by the *Illuminata* – the Daughters of
the Light – or by the *Saguis Domini*, or Blood
Lords.  She would be easily bent to the devices
of darker magics, with that uncontrolled temper
of hers.  That thought made him frown, concern
washing through him.  Geoff was right, this
woman needed training, to protect herself.  He
just wasn't sure he was the one to do it.

Ah, there she was.  Meg was seated at a city
bus stop, her elbows propped on her knees and
her face buried in her hands.  She was swaying
back and forth like a reed in high winds, and her
slumped shoulders trembled.  No surprise there.
It had to be below freezing out here, and she
wasn't wearing anything but that ridiculously
threadbare waitress' uniform.

As Mac approached silently, he realized she
wasn't just trying to stay warm.  Meg Tempest
was sobbing, the harsh sound muffled by the
hands covering her face, as if she couldn't bear
to let even the strangers passing on the street see
her cry.  Suddenly, she didn't look furious or
fearless, anymore.  She looked small, lost, and so
vulnerable Mac felt a corresponding tightness in
his chest that surprised him.

He wasn't, by nature, a compassionate
person.  The only person he'd ever felt any real
tenderness for was Ysabet, who had wrapped
him around her tiny finger the day she'd been
born.  He'd only just met this woman, how was
it she stirred that same desire to protect within
him his innocent sister did, and yet roused a
heat that was distinctly *un*brotherly?

He didn't want to think about that, Mac told himself as he sat beside her on the bench and slipped off his leather jacket, draping it over her hunched, trembling shoulders. Meg jumped, her head rising sharply.

"You'll freeze, sitting here like that."

A scowl covered her face, and she pushed the jacket away. "What are you doing here?"

He merely shrugged, unable to explain why he'd followed her, or the impulses the silky, lightly accented purr of her voice stirred within him. He wanted to cover the space between them and taste those pouty lips, to find out if they were as sweet as her fresh face promised, or as hot as those snapping honey-brown eyes. He wouldn't do it, of course. He had an ulterior motive that prohibited him from such liberties. He winced inwardly. There was no way he could ever let Meg find out about his bet with Geoff, with her temper, she'd geld him first, and *maybe* ask questions after.

The silence stretched as he debated what to tell her, and Mac got the distinct impression Meg was trying to ignore his presence. He nearly chuckled at the insolence in her stiff posture, it was rare when a woman managed to ignore him when he wanted her attention. However, Meg looked like she was going to give it her best shot. And she was shivering again.

Finally, with a sigh, Mac reached over and resettled the leather jacket around her shoulders, his fingertips brushing against the soft skin of her neck. A jolt went through him at that contact. Gods, she was so delicate on the outside, even if her eyes flashed with a core of solid steel.

"I was serious, you know," he finally said quietly. "I do have a proposition for you."

"Go away." Her voice was stone cold, slicing through him like a knife.

He sighed in exasperation. He wasn't sure if he wanted to train this woman, kiss her, or murder her. Spirit of Shadow, she was infuriating! "Just hear me out, lass. I promise you, it'll be worth your while."

"Why *should* I?" She whipped her gaze his way, her ale-colored eyes snapping with rage. "I don't even have that lousy job, anymore, thanks to you."

"You don't need it."

Her laugh was swift and bitter, her glare hardening with icy contempt. "Shows what you know! That job was my *life*!"

He snorted in disbelief. She couldn't possibly be serious. "That wasn't living. You looked miserable."

"Maybe," she admitted grudgingly, before her face turned away, and she heaved a dispirited sigh. "But it was all I had left."

The grim resignation of those words pricked Mac's heart, surprising him again. When he'd first seen her, she'd looked haggard and unkempt, and he'd assumed she was an untidy person. Could he have been wrong about her? Could she be hanging onto a semblance of normal life by a thread? Shame, an entirely new feeling for him, trickled through Mac. She was struggling to maintain normal life, and he'd belittled her efforts with his arrogance.

He'd never encountered poverty, before, not like this. He'd assumed this dimension's poor were such by choice, choosing sloth over prosperity. However, Meg Tempest looked worn down by life, as if her every dream had been shattered by misfortune and poverty. An ache stirred in Mac's soul that surprised him in its intensity. He longed to see this weary woman smile.

"What of your happiness?" He enquired quietly. "Don't you dream of a better life than that?"

Her face remained turned away from him, but the shadows of bitterness and resignation cloaked her as she muttered, "That's none of your business."

"Ah, but that's where you're wrong," he said easily. He tipped his head back, to watch the snowflakes swirl down onto the bus shelter's Plexiglas roof, and smiled. "You see, Meg, my pet, I can show you how to make all your dreams come true."

Her spine stiffened, and Mac cast a swift glance of surprise her direction as she loosed a sarcastic laugh. "Yeah, right. And I'm the Queen of Sheba."

He raised a brow at her caustic tone, he wasn't about to let her goad him into an argument. "If you wish, though I warn you, you wouldn't want her job."

His eyes traveled over her slowly, and his blood stirred as he wondered what she hid beneath that shapeless uniform. He drew a deep breath, and caught the subtle scent of her, like warm cinnamon. His chest tightened as he murmured, "You don't seem the regal type."

Her lips flickered as her head turned ever so slightly toward him, and Mac sucked in a breath of freezing winter air, his lungs burning with the sudden cold. He'd never considered how erotic a smile could be, until now. His heart pumped hard, his blood flowing so fast he felt light-headed. All this over the thought of seeing Meg smile. If he were able to think past the rush of lust through his veins, the mere idea would probably be absurd.

Her expression settled again, and the brief flicker of a smile that haunted her lips fled. Mac subdued a flash of disappointment. This fascination with Meg had to stop, he couldn't lust after a woman he didn't even know. Besides, he couldn't train a woman he was lusting after. That was a recipe for disaster.

"Okay," Meg finally broke the strained silence between them with a short sigh. Her honey-brown eyes narrowed on him as she tossed back a lock of dark, curly hair. "I'll bite. How do you intend to make all my dreams come true?"

"*I* won't," he answered quietly as he forced his eyes closed against the sight of her tempting lips and mesmerizing eyes. Tipping his head back, he drew in deep breaths of cold air and ordered his body to subside. It paid him no mind, and he winced at the throb of painful desire against the zipper of his jeans. He could order the span of night and day, reorder the shadows of time itself. It came as an unwelcome surprise to learn his own body was apparently not his to control. Right now, it was under the spell of a dark-haired seductress with eyes a man could drown in, and...

*Dammit, no!* He scowled as he yanked his mind off that dangerous path. He couldn't want Meg. He had a bet to win, a bet his sister's future was riding on. With a sharply indrawn breath, he felt his lungs burn with the cold, even as he rasped, "What I will do is teach you how to bend and shape the shadows of time and space, to bring the images of your dreams and desires into your reality. I'll show you how to turn the wishes of the past into a part of your present, and give you the means to bring the world of dreams to life."

Her eyes were wary, when he finally risked a glance at her, and he could see she was weighing every word he'd said. Mac contained the wry smile that tugged at his lips. Clearly, Meg Tempest was more cautious than her actions so far had led him to believe. That was a good thing. Cautious people could be taught to control their own impulses. He began to feel better about the idea of training her. Geoff was right, Meg had definite potential.

"Only the past and present?" She finally asked in the sexy purr that made the hairs on his neck stand on end, and Mac clenched his jaw against the heat rushing through him. "What about the future?"

"The future is a mutable realm," he

managed with a shake of his head as he tipped his head back again and closed his eyes. "It is a realm forbidden to the *Sgàil Ealdhainean*."

She blinked at him. "Skaal Elaanen?" Her tongue tripped over the words. "What's that?"

He slanted her a brief look. "The Shadow Arts."

Her ale-colored eyes widened like a cornered doe's, and a small gasp left her. "Shadow Arts? As in," her voice dropped to a breathless whisper, "black magic?"

Mac laughed at the absurdity of the comparison. He'd learned a lot about these people called Americans, in his time here. They, and most of their world, were so misinformed about magic, they jumped in fright at anything they didn't understand. So quick to point a finger, or blame a system of beliefs. They believed everything they didn't understand was evil. Small wonder the *Saguis Domini* so enjoyed preying upon this realm. All that fear would be an irresistible draw to those who fed off such emotions. Shaking his head, he met Meg's troubled gaze with a reassuring smile. "No, *leannan*. The *Sgàil Ealdhainean*," he murmured as he gathered the muted shadow of the shelter, forming it within his hands, "are in a very different realm."

*****

Meg gasped in surprise as the man beside her opened his hands, to offer her a delicate, snow-white lily. Disbelief sparked in her as, awed, she stretched out one hand to touch the fragile blossom, expecting it to vanish beneath her trembling fingertips. She blinked, and gasped again, as her fingers skimmed satin-soft petals. It was real!

"How…" She raised stunned eyes to his copper-bright gaze, and knew what it was like to free-fall. God, she'd never seen eyes so deep, before! It was like… like staring into a campfire, she decided as she watched the light flicker and dance in his eyes. She wasn't sure what was real, and what was the shadow of illusion. Her body tingled with heat, stirred to life by those eyes, and her mouth was dry as dust. Her tongue darted over her lips, and the flames in his eyes shot higher. Swallowing jerkily, she cleared her throat before, in a husky murmur, she managed, "How did you do that?"

"Come with me," he offered softly. "Come with me, sweet Meg, and learn what you just saw is merely a parlor trick, compared to what's all around us, waiting to be shaped and molded by your dreams."

She was tempted. Hell, if she was honest with herself, the idea of going anywhere with a man as sexy as this one *more* than tempted her. An image flashed through her mind, of her and him, tangled in a twist of shadowy satin, naked and hungry only for each other. She gasped as heat drenched her body in needy sensation, even as a voice – the same voice she'd heard for as long as she could remember, and never revealed to a soul – whispered in her head. *Choose wisely.*

Meg resisted the urge to roll her eyes. Some help that voice was, she had no idea what was wise, right now. She only knew what *stupid* would be, and agreeing blindly with this deal would be that. Her parents were proof enough of the stupidity impulsiveness bred. Meg wasn't about to repeat their mistakes. So, drawing away from the encompassing warmth of Alasdair MacCorran's eyes, and his scent, she studied him, her common sense overriding her innate curiosity. After all, she was well acquainted with the story of Faust, and, as sexy and charming as *this* devil was, Meg Tempest was nobody's fool.

"What's the catch?"

He sat back with a sound that was half sigh, half chuckle, and his hands fell to rest against muscular, denim-encased thighs. *Black* jeans, no less. Her heart stumbled. God, her bad boy radar was tingling like crazy. This man radiated sex appeal like a shadowy aura, and it drew her. She imagined it drew a lot of women. Like danger, that aura was probably some kind of aphrodisiac.

After a long moment, he finally met her gaze steadily and, in that blood-tingling, deep brogue, admitted, "There are rules, of course."

Meg smirked. Of course. There were *always* rules. Even Faust had learned that, although he'd learned far too late to change his mind. Meg wasn't about to make that mistake. She'd learned a long time ago nothing worth having came for free. So, cocking him a curious glance, she enquired, "And those rules would be?"

He reached up, did something to the shadow above them, and plucked a thin volume from the air. Meg blinked as he handed it to her, and her eyes dropped to the cover. Uh-oh. This was bound to be trouble. She shot him a wary look. "*Discipulus Optibri*? I hate to break this to you, but I don't know Latin."

He lifted one dark brow, and she saw humor dancing in his bronze eyes. "Really? Who said that was Latin?"

Annoyance plowed aside the heat of a moment ago. She glared at him. "Don't insult my intelligence."

The humor in his eyes spread to his lips, curving them up in a grin that put a rakish slash in his right cheek and sent her libido skyrocketing again. Okay, so not only did he have a voice like Sean Connery, but he had a grin that put Harrison Ford to shame, too. She could handle that. She was a grown woman, for God's sake, not some star-struck teen!

"It *is* a form of Latin," he agreed in that husky brogue, "and a test. Something in you knows that's Latin, and that means you have the genetic ancestry to learn magic. Don't worry, the rest of the book is in your native tongue."

She nodded, even as uneasiness slid through her. He'd handed her a rulebook. She wasn't very good with rules. However, for the chance to make her dreams come true... "What are the most important rules I need to remember?"

His eyes raked over her with a searing look

that made her feel naked from the soul out. Meg shifted as restless heat spiked through her. God, what was he doing to her? She'd never responded to a man like this, before.

"There are three rules you must abide by, to be my apprentice." His eyes met hers again. "Rule One: Whether you accept my offer or not, you can't tell anyone about this deal, or what you saw here. This is the most important rule of magic, Ms. Tempest– secrecy. The last time someone broke the *Pactus Silentium*, scores of *Thorolfkin* were brutally massacred by *Contra Magi* who were terrified of what they didn't understand."

Meg nodded. "That's what the Wiccans call the 'Burning Time,' right?"

"No," he replied, frowning. "Though I'm sure a few *Draoi* and *Magi* like myself died amidst that idiocy. Not nearly as many as the number of *Thorolfkin* who died at the hands of the hunters." His gaze narrowed on her, his bronze eyes piercingly clear. "You must agree to this rule. If you do not, I'll be forced to blank your memory of our entire conversation, and you'll return to exactly where you were before we met."

She shuddered at the thought. Go back to that? No, thanks.

"All right. I agree, I'll never tell anyone." It was an easy promise to make, after all. She didn't intend to ever try to describe anything she'd just seen. Not even if she actually had someone to tell, which she didn't. Today ranked right up there with the voice in her head. If she told anyone, they'd have her in a straightjacket before she could blink.

He smiled, his easy demeanor of a moment ago returning. "Rule Two: You'll have to come live with me, in my cabin, for the next month. In that time, you'll learn wonders the likes of which you've only dreamed, but you must remain until the Second of January, by your calendar. No matter what you see, or how unbearable you believe the training to be, you must see the month out."

Meg froze. That was one hell of a catch. He was asking her to make an agreement of blind faith – something she'd never been much good at. She had no idea what might happen. The most exposure she'd ever had to magic – excluding to lily and book tricks she'd just seen – was a very disastrous encounter with a *Ouija* board, thanks to her ex-roommate, Shannon Taylor. Then again, she realized with a wry twist of her lips, Alasdair MacCorran was setting these rules on blind faith, too. They could *both* live to regret Rule Two.

She looked up to tell him as much, and found herself held captive by those compelling bronze eyes. Her pulse stuttered on cue, and her blood simmered with raw lust. A slow, wicked smile tugged at her lips. Surely, spending a month alone with a hottie like Alasdair MacCorran couldn't be *all* bad.

## CHAPTER FOUR

Mac gazed down into the hunger swirling in Meg's honey-brown eyes, and fought the uneasy feeling he was in big trouble. Bad enough he found it increasingly difficult to banish the sudden fantasy of stripping off that shapeless waitress' uniform to see if her nipples were puckered from the cold. His imagination painted images of warming those stiff, chilled tips with his mouth, and Mac groaned as uncomfortable pressure built against his fly. The hot desire melting Meg's eyes only made his predicament worse. It was torment to know he wasn't alone in this crazy attraction.

Meg's tongue darted out again, moistening her lightly tinted lips, and Mac heard the roar of blood in his ears as it all rushed south, fast. He had to shift, to ease the press of his jeans against his erection. Spirit of Shadow, he wanted this woman! He craved her taste, and the feel of her flesh, with a lust he hadn't felt in too long, if ever. Great. Mac muttered a curse as he faced the truth. The only woman he'd actually *wanted* in years was a woman he *couldn't* want, if she accepted his offer.

"Mr. MacCorran?" The silky purr of her voice slid over him, and Mac felt its erotic pull clear to the roots of his hair. That light, exotic accent of Meg's was more potent than any aphrodisiac.

"Mac," he corrected her in a hoarse mutter, when he could finally find his voice again.

One slim, dark brow lifted over those amazing eyes, and Mac held his breath until she murmured, "Mac, is there anything else?"

He blinked, nonplussed, and realized he couldn't recall what they were discussing. What manner of witch *was* this woman? "Else?"

Humor flickered in her eyes, and a small smile touched her lips. "Rules, Mac. You were telling me the rules. Are there any more?"

Only one, he remembered with no small regret. Only *the* most important law of magical balance, and why there was a taboo on training the opposite sex. It'd been drummed into Mac from infancy, and he'd never forgotten it, not until Meg's honey-brown eyes had snared him, and refused to let go. With a sigh, and a shift to ease the flare of lust, he cleared his throat. "There is one more rule."

She sighed, and faced him grimly. "Important?"

"Very."

"All right. What is it?" The resignation in her voice made him wish even more that it wasn't so important. He wanted her to be happy, he realized with a start. Even more, he wanted to be the one who made her happy. With a swallowed curse, he steeled himself to meet her eyes. She wasn't going to like this any more than he did.

"No matter what, there can be no sexual contact between mentor and apprentice."

*****

Well, damn.  Meg slumped back against the hard plastic bench as disappointment rushed through her.  A bleak laugh stuck in her throat as she replayed his words.  Why was she so surprised?  Mac was the first man she'd met in a long time who stirred her imagination, and her blood, and the *only* one, that she could remember, who made her feel naked and tingly with nothing more than a glance of those bronze eyes.  So, naturally, Murphy's Law must strike again, and make him off-limits.  Her luck hadn't changed.

She sighed dispiritedly.  Damn, damn, damn.  And she'd been looking forward to the chance to jump his bones.  Her gaze slid over him, and her body tingled with demanding want.  Double damn.

A small, wry grin tugged at her lips, then.  The last man who'd stirred her at all, Carl, had turned out to be gay.  Maybe she should just be glad her sexual-orientation radar was finally working right, because there was no way in hell Mac was gay.  With those bronze eyes of his hot enough to melt steel, not to mention every bone in her body, and his brogue-laden voice husky with desire, even the infamous Murphy couldn't convince her Alasdair MacCorran wasn't interested.  This man wanted her, and he wanted her bad.

Meg's grin broke loose, as mischief shot through her.  It'd been too long since she's played any kind of attraction game.  Men usually didn't see her, and the ones who did were old perverts, or whack-jobs. From what she'd seen so far, Mac didn't appear to be either one. And he'd offered her the chance to live in close quarters with him for a whole month. Hot damn! She eyed him again, and her smile bloomed. Oh, yeah. Rules or no rules, if she agreed to this deal, she'd have Mac to herself until the Second of January. She might not be a femme fatal, but Meg had learned a thing or two from her former roommate, who worked as an exotic dancer. She had a whole month to bring Mac to his knees, and make him bend that final rule of his until it broke.

Meg smirked. Okay, so she was horny, and she had a healthy imagination. She wasn't about to make any apologies for that. Mac was prime beefcake, and she couldn't think of a better way for them to both get what they really wanted than a simple, no-strings affair. She wouldn't have to worry about falling for someone like Mac. He was way out of her league.

She shifted as she drew in a steadying breath that, thanks to the jacket he'd draped over her shoulders, smelled of leather and the elusively intoxicating scent of Mac's body heat. A tingle of awareness shot through her, dampening her sex. Yeah, she was *more* than ready for that affair, as long as it involved lots of hot sex.

With a grin, she met Mac's eyes and stuck out her hand. "You've convinced me. I'm game, Mac."

He returned her smile, his eyes warm, as he engulfed her hand with his, lifting it to his lips in smooth European fashion. "You won't regret it, *leannan*. I promise you that."

She chuckled, to cover the flutter of her pulse at the feel of his warm skin against hers. "No, but you might."

He cocked a brow at her as he released her hand. "How do you figure?"

"Murphy's Law," she quipped as she bent her head, already flipping through the book he'd handed her as she sought to avoid meeting his gaze. "Ask anyone, Mac. I'm a walking minefield."

*****

*Rule #1 for the aspiring magical apprentice: Do not believe you are in control.*

Great. Meg sighed as the first line of the thin volume popped out at her. More rules. Not that she was a rule-breaker, by nature, but she and rules didn't exactly get along. She'd learned her lesson a long time ago. The more rules she was given, the greater the chance disaster would strike, and they were already up to four rules.

She wasn't all that worried about the rule, itself. Control wasn't something Meg was used to having, anyway. With a wry shake of her head, she glanced at the man seated beside her as she flipped through the rest of the book. So far, she hadn't seen *his* rules anywhere.

"If these are the rules for apprenticeship,

why don't I see yours anywhere?"

He rose to his feet, offering her a hand up in a very old-fashioned manner. Meg smiled to herself, and had to admit she liked the way he always acted so chivalrously. What woman wouldn't want to be treated like a queen?

"Rule One is under the chapter on 'Training *Intiro*.' Rule Three is covered in the next chapter, in great detail."

Really? Meg's pulse sped up at just the thought. There was a whole chapter on the no-sex rule? That meant there had to be a loophole. She quirked a curious brow at him careful not to appear too eager for an explanation. "What kind of great detail?"

He straightened, his expression cold, even though his eyes blazed. "It defines what is and is not, according to the ancient laws of the *Illuminata*, considered sexual relations."

"Like what?"

His jaw clenched so tight she could see the tic in it, before he rasped, "In your case, *nothing*."

Meg bit back a grin as he stressed the final word, and she realized she was testing his control, as well as her own. It felt good to know she rattled him as much as he affected her. "Why? Not interested?"

He groaned, and muttered something beneath his breath before he warned, "Meg, this is inappropriate…"

"Why?" She blinked innocently at him as they started toward the coffee shop. "We're not doing anything, Mac. I'm just trying to understand the rules."

"You know damned well what you're doing, *leannan*," he bit out the words through clenched teeth.

She bit back a grin, and pasted on her most innocent expression. "I'm just trying to understand the rules of our relationship."

He stopped abruptly, and Meg gasped as his gaze clashed with hers, and the heat of it sent a lightning bolt straight through her.

"The rules are simple," he rasped in that deep, body-tingling brogue. "We don't have a relationship. And there will be no sex."

She let out an exasperated breath as she saw the hard-held conviction in his eyes. Damn the man. He wasn't going to let her get around him on any of it. "So, sex is out completely, huh?"

His jaw tightened until she was sure it would crack in half. "Aye."

"Geeze." She shook her head in amusement. Mac thought he had the market cornered on stubborn? He had no idea how far she'd go to get what she wanted, and right now, all she wanted was *him*. She wanted him between her thighs, where she ached for his attention. And she'd get him, too, eventually. He couldn't hold out forever. "Either you guys have ice water in place of blood, or magicians all have blue balls."

"Meg," he warned gruffly, his voice cracking slightly. "Don't go there."

"Why not?"

He headed grimly toward the coffee shop,

and Meg's eyes narrowed as she realized he was trying to ignore her. She blinked. Mac was moving in stiff, jerky strides that seemed totally at odds with his smooth, dark presence. Concern washed through her, displacing her anger and the ache to feel him inside her. Did he have an injury she hadn't noticed? Maybe something that prevented him from taking what they both wanted?

"Are you okay?" She blurted as she hurried to catch up with him, and nearly ran into his back as he stopped, turning his head to shoot her a confused glance. Blushing furiously at her gaff, she rushed on, "I noticed you're walking a little stiffly, and—"

A raspy laugh, and a muttered oath in a language she didn't understand broke his lips, and Meg suddenly found herself backed up against the wall of the nearest building as Mac's mouth crushed over hers in a hungry, demanding kiss. His big body wedged against hers from chest to thighs and she felt the thick bulge beneath his jeans grind into her abdomen. Meg gasped, her eyes going wide in surprise, as she realized *exactly* why he'd been moving so stiffly. The man was rock-hard!

Dampness drenched her sex as blood rushed to her erogenous zones at the thought of having Mac's hard cock buried in her throbbing body, and every nerve ending in her screamed, *yes*! She groaned with the heat flashing through her, and burrowed her fingers into his thick, dark hair as she lifted herself against him, wrapping her legs around his waist and rubbing to create delicious friction. His tongue danced inside her mouth, a seductive, shadowy game of dare that brought every cell in her body alive with need. Goddamn, did he know how to kiss!

Boldly, Meg returned his exploration, turning the seductive tempo into a sultry tango as she shifted her hips against his body, and felt the hard bulge of him settle against her sex. God, yes. She rocked against him, and he growled in response, the sound a rumble in his chest that surprised Meg. She'd never heard a man growl before. It shivered along her nerve endings like heat lightning, tightening her nipples and sending another drenching wave through her womb. God, that sound was sexy as hell.

Mac broke the kiss then, his chest heaving as he stared down at her. His eyes were slightly glazed, but bright with hunger. Her breath backed up in her throat as she gazed back into that hungry glow, even as he muttered, "Great Stars…"

"Mmm." Meg purred, and rubbed sinuously against him as she wondered what it would take to talk Mac into retiring to somewhere a little more private than the Seattle streets to finish what they'd started. Not much, to judge by the thickness resting against her pelvis. Good God, if the man was even *half* the size that hard ridge promised, she'd melt from rapture. A husky chuckle worked loose from her throat at the image of melting into a boneless puddle at his feet. "How does this not break Rule Three, again?"

He swore again in that strange, melodic language, and abruptly stepped away from her, leaving Meg feeling cold. "This is insane."

No, that was what he was driving *her*, Meg decided peevishly. Frustration, due in no small part to the unfulfilled ache in her nether regions, flashed through Meg. Damn it, he couldn't do this to her! Yanking her chin up, she glared at him as she challenged, "Why? Because you want me? What the hell's wrong with that?"

He loosed a sharp bark of laughter, its vehemence startling Meg. "Because I'm you're mentor, *leannan*. I'm not *allowed* to want you."

She stared after him, slack-jawed, as he turned toward *Hole in the Wall*'s parking lot, his expression bleak. He was already several strides ahead of her when the shock finally wore off, and she was forced to jog to catch up with him. As she fell into step beside him, she regarded him curiously. Mac didn't seem the type to deny himself for the sake of a rulebook. "Look, I don't know about you, but that rule sucks, from where I'm standing. So, let's just throw out the rulebook on that one, and make it up as we go along."

"No," he returned grimly as they reached the edge of the parking lot.

"Why not?"

He stopped beside a vintage black and chrome motorcycle emblazoned with the famous winged "M" that denoted a British-manufactured Matchless. "Because some rules can't be broken, or ignored. That's one of them."

"C'mon, Mac!    That rule smacks of Medieval, here…"

He shot her a dark look. "If you can't abide by the basic bylaws, you'll never manage the control necessary to meet the challenges presented by magic."

She rolled her eyes.   Clearly, he wasn't giving up on this one without a fight.   Fine. She'd prove her point, eventually.   With a sigh, she offered, "I guess I should have figured that one out."

His lips quirked.    "That was too easy. What're you plotting?"

Uncomfortable with his perceptiveness, Meg shifted, and then shivered as a gust of wind stung her legs.  It was time for a subject change, before she froze to death.  "Where's your car? I'm freezing, here."

"Lift your arms," he instructed softly, as he drew the leather jacket from her shoulders. Another gust of icy wind hit her just then, raising gooseflesh and puckering her nipples with the chill.

She heard a strangled sound, and glanced up to find Mac's bronze gaze fixed on her breasts, that slumberous, sexy light flashing in them again.  Hmm.  It appeared there were some advantages to not owning a bra.  She shivered as heat and cold plunged through her simultaneously, and she ached for his touch.

"Mac?"

"Hmm?"  His gaze was glued to her body, even as one dark brow rose in query.  Meg shifted.   She felt restless and achy, and she wanted to just scream, *Touch me!* But she was too afraid he wouldn't, if she did.

"Mac, I'm freezing."

It wasn't completely true, but it was enough to snap Mac out of whatever fantasy glazed his eye. Grim-faced, he reached out and slipped the leather jacket up over her arms. In one firm motion, he pulled it closed over her body and zipped it. He never said a word, though, and as he turned toward the bike, trepidation shot through Meg. He didn't...

"Mac, is that *yours*?"

He flicked her a glance, and nodded. "And 'that' is a 1967 Matchless G80CS, custom restored and painted. It's a classic, Meg."

"It's a *motorcycle*." Meg fought the sudden hammer of her pulse, hoping like hell Mac couldn't tell what bothered her most about that fact. There was no way she was getting on that thing, not with Mac.

He cocked one dark brow at her. "Is there a problem?"

"I...um..." Meg flushed, averting her gaze. No way she was going to tell him motorcycles terrified her, because then she'd have to explain *why*, and that thought was mortifying. How could she ever explain her bizarre, blood-heating dreams to this man without seeming slutty? She couldn't, plain and simple. So she lied, instead. "No. No problem at all."

His eyes ran over her assessingly, and his expression softened briefly, before he swung one leg over the leather seat and nodded toward the bike. "Hop on."

Meg's eyes fixed on the leather seat, and she swallowed hard as Mac's invitation sizzled through her. Torrid images and sensations flashed through her, of hot, thrumming leather against bare flesh, and the deep counterpoint of —

She closed her eyes and bit back a groan as she clamped her thighs together in an effort to stave off the quivering in her sex. There was no way she was getting on that bike with Mac, not with *that* dream pulsing in her head.

"Meg?" Mac's deep, concerned voice broke through her wild thoughts, and she flushed. He must think her the worst kind of coward. He had no idea what she was thinking.

*Get on the damned bike, Tempest,* she commanded herself sternly as she forced her feet to move. She was starting to freeze, her legs already numb from the cold. Now wasn't the time to debate the wisdom of sexual fantasy against practical consideration. If the Matchless was her only means of getting somewhere warm, then she was just going to have to deal with it.

She moved resolutely to the bike, and stopped, chagrin sweeping through her as another problem struck her. "Umm… Mac?"

She watched his eyes sweep over her, and saw comprehension dawn as his bronze gaze reached the hem of her uniform skirt. A slow smile spread over his lips as he raised his eyes to hers again, and she saw laughter dancing there.

"Might get a tad drafty. I think you'll live, though."

"Try a *lot* drafty," she muttered, even as she felt another blush heat up her cheeks. Damn it, she hated that she blushed so easily. "Mac, I don't…"

His grin widened at her hesitance, and she wished she had something heavy to throw at him. This *wasn't* funny, damn him!

"Scared of a cold seat?" He asked with a devilish gleam in his eyes. Oh, yeah. He was *all* bad boy, now, complete with black leather and attitude to spare. Only, it wasn't cute or melting, anymore. Irritation snapped through her shyness.

"Yes. Dammit, Mac, I don't wear underwear!"

He tensed, as if she'd slapped him, and his grin died completely as horror filled his eyes and he croaked, "You're kidding."

He sounded as if he was begging her to confirm his words. She wished she could, she didn't like this little show-and-tell any more than he did. Talk about fatally embarrassing. With a forced smile, she shrugged.

"'Fraid not. My parents are of the 'freedom in every form' school of thought. I haven't worn underwear since my third birthday."

He groaned, and she watched his eyes close as he slumped on the bike. She wasn't sure what to say. She'd never had to face such a thunderstruck look at that admission before. A long, uncomfortable silence stretched between them, and Meg shifted from foot to foot in an effort to keep warm as she debated how best to end the silence.

"Damn." The short, sharp oath in Mac's deep voice brought her eyes to his face just in time to see his jaw clench. His burning eyes raked over her, nearly melting Meg on the spot, before he swung off of the bike and rasped, "We'll take your car."

Meg started, and nearly laughed. Talk about presumption! "I don't have one."

He froze, his wary eyes glued on her face as he searched for something. She met his gaze, unflinching. Damn, she hated this. Then, after a moment, Mac's eyes closed and he groaned in disbelief. "*Please* tell me this is a joke."

A smile twitched at her lips. Was she actually *scaring* him with her honesty? If so, it was only fair, since he'd imposed that damned rule on her libido.

"Wish I could. My car died two weeks ago, and I can't afford to get it fixed. I'm reliant on public transportation." She offered him an apologetic grin. "Why else would I be sitting in the freezing cold without a coat?"

He muttered something beneath his breath, and settled back onto the bike. "Get on. We'll manage."

Manage what was the question. But, rather than argue a point she had no leverage to win, Meg swallowed back her discomfort and did as instructed. She tensed as she settled onto the bike, gasping as the cold leather touched her hot skin, and sensations from that erotic dream returned. Oh, was this ever a bad idea.

*****

Mac heard the woman behind him loose a tiny, involuntary gasp, and clenched his jaw against the fantasies that little sound roused. Great Orion's Belt, he'd already been so aroused he wasn't sure he could steer this thing *before* she let slip she was as bare as the day she was born beneath his jacket and that thin uniform. As icy as the wind was, he barely felt it, his blood so hot he was actually sweating.

Eyes closed, he fought images of laying Meg out over the seat and lifting that ridiculous scrap of a skirt to watch the gooseflesh bloom and hear her moan as he opened her to the cold wind. The icy breeze would chill her dampness, and he could warm it with his mouth, sucking heat back into that sensitive flesh as she arched and twisted —

"Mac?" Her quiet, lightly accented voice burst through his fantasy, and he dragged his mind back to the present with a suppressed groan. Great Shadows, he was in trouble! His cock was ready to burst with the need to be in her, and, as he felt her shift behind him, he had to stifle another groan. Every touch burned him, as her bare inner thighs brushed his jeans-clad hips, and her – Sweet Shadows help him! – bare heat pressed against his backside. She was going to drive him crazy. "Are we going?"

Mac bit down on a harsh oath. No, they weren't going, yet, but if she moved like that even once more, they were both going to be *coming*, fast. With another bitten-off oath, Mac battled down the inappropriate image of having hot, wild sex with his new apprentice. Maybe she was right, maybe this whole thing was a bad idea. However, he didn't have much of a choice. He'd made his bet with Geoff, and his deal with Meg. Both were binding.

Grimly, Mac twisted the key and throttled the G80 into motion. The sooner he got this ride over with, the sooner he could get this woman out of sight and off his mind, before he gave in to urges that would get him into trouble. Like seducing a woman he wasn't allow to have.

*****

Shadows shifted and stretched as the motorcycle roared past the bus stop, and a figure slowly solidified, crouching to lift the discarded, ice-covered flutter of white. Cupping the frozen blossom in his hand, he breathed on it, and sparks flashed, before the fragile lily disintegrated into ashes. Breathing in, he savored the shadow-scents of the woman who'd held it. *Meg*.

Finnagas Crawford smiled to himself as he watched the ashes stir and blow away on the cold air. He was getting close now. He could smell her sweet, innocent fragrance. Damara had been clever to hide her. He'd given up years of his life searching for her.

*Ah, little Meg, you can't hide from me now.* He'd spent too many years searching every magical enclave and school for that scent, and the child to whom it'd belonged. When he'd felt her power bloom, for the first time last year, he'd come to this backward dimension in search of her. With Meg, he'd have the means to his revenge. All he had to do was convince her to aid him, and, with the power in her blood, he'd have access to the Twelve Gates of the *Strata*. All he had to do, now, was lure her away from the MacCorrans.

## CHAPTER FIVE

They'd only been on the road for an hour, and she already wanted to scream with frustration. Clamping her jaw shut, Meg scrunched her eyes closed and counted silently in an effort to stave off the itchy, restless feeling in her lower body. Every minute that passed was a torturous combination of pleasure and pain, as sensual heat and numbing cold flew through her in waves. Biting her lip hard, she rested her cheek against the solid warmth of Mac's back, her fingers wrapped in the belt loops of his jeans and his scent, as elusive and dangerous as a shadow, filling her lungs. God, she'd never known a man could smell so damned good before.

She wasn't freezing at any rate. Mac's big body cut most of the cold wind, with just enough flowing over her bare thighs and legs to make her skin tingle with the chill. The bike throbbed beneath her, and she bit back a moan of exquisite torment as her nipples hardened from the sensual assault that knifed through her womb. She wanted to hook her thumbs into Mac's belt loops and splay her hands. She needed to know he was as turned on as she was. But she didn't dare. If she was right, and he was, they'd no doubt end up wrapped around one of the towering, snow-covered pines that lined the road. And if she was wrong... Well, she didn't want to know. She didn't think she could bear the thought of being alone in this insane attraction.

Her eyes squeezed even tighter as she hugged him tight, unsure how much more she could take. She wanted to beg him to stop the bike and screw her until the ache went away, but Mac had made it clear he didn't intend to do anything of the kind. She wanted to ask how much longer and where they were going, but knew any attempt would be pointless. The wind would simply whip the words away. It would be a futile effort to attempt either plea, and Meg had given up on futile efforts fifteen years ago. So, instead, she just held tightly to Mac and let the wind take her flyaway hair, like a dark flame, as she rested her cheek against his back and fantasized what it would feel like to be straddling Mac's hard body, instead of this noise machine, that rock-hard erection she'd felt earlier buried deep in her. It was a dream she intended to make reality, someday soon. Before she went completely nuts.

*****

Mac pulled the G80 to the shoulder of the road as they reached the junction of the old, dirt logging trail that led to his cabin, his brow furrowed in concern. Meg had been shifting and muttering strangely for the past twenty minutes, ever since they'd hit Fall City. He was afraid she was sick, or suffering from exposure. Not everyone could handle icy winter wind on a moving bike, and she wasn't wearing much to cut the chill.

Turning slightly, he tried to see her face, but that was impossible with her burrowed against him like she was, her small, curvy body melded to his back. All he could see was a tousle of dark, curly hair and a flash of black leather from his jacket. He glanced down as he felt her muscles flex, and saw the purplish gooseflesh of her bare thigh. Merciful Spirits, she must be freezing!

Trying to warm her, he laid his hand on her thigh, rubbing briskly. Instantly, Meg moaned, and her hips flexed against his backside. Her fingers spread wide, brushing against the hard-on he'd been sporting every since he'd made the mistake of kissing her. The cold air would have subdued that, if she hadn't been pressed up against him for the past forty-five minutes. Now, as her fingers slid over him through the denim, he groaned, his fingers digging into her cold, bare thigh in warning.

"Meg…"

She stirred against him, and he turned enough that he could see her luminous eyes in the gathering dusk. He sucked in a sharp breath. Sweet Shadows, this woman had night-eyes! Aside from the *Thorolfkin* and the *Werefolk*, only the *Illuminata* had the luminous eyes that allowed them to see as well at night as in day. If she'd been *Thorolfkin* or Were, Geoff would have known and said. *Meg* would have known. Which meant… Mac groaned. He was lusting after an *Illuminata*? What had Geoff gotten him into now?

"Mac," her soft, breathy voice brushed over

him, making him throb with the need to bury himself in her. Great Spirit of Shadow hide him. *Illuminata* or not, he wanted to bang her brains out, here and now.

"Mac," she breathed his name again, the desperation in her tone drawing his gaze. He found himself drowning in ale-colored eyes that glowed from within. "Mac, fuck me. Please."

The raw need in her voice nearly undid him. He wanted to. Spirit of Shadow knew, he wanted nothing more than to haul her around, drape her over this bike, and make all his most wicked fantasies into reality. All his *inappropriate* fantasies.

Mac swore beneath his breath and closed his eyes as he yanked his face forward. Meg was his apprentice. By the rules of magic, her verbal agreement back in Seattle had made it a signed deal. And Geoff was right when he'd said Mac wasn't a rebel. He might flaunt tradition on occasion, but he'd never break an established, written law. A man not teaching women was a practical tradition passed down orally. While it might gain scorn from some more traditional practitioners, it wouldn't get him an official reprimand or banishment by the *Illuminata*. However, seducing his apprentice – especially if she turned out to be a daughter of the *Illuminata* – was a sure-fire way to end up before the High Council.

"We're almost there," he bit out the words, gunning the bike into motion again.

"Mac?" She sounded confused, and more than a little hurt, and he hated that. But, dammit, she knew the rules. As badly as he wanted her, he couldn't have her. Not until after *Luna Ascesa*. After that, all bets were off.

*****

Five minutes later, Mac brought the bike to a stop again and sighed with relief. Finally, he could put some space between himself and the tempting little witch he'd agreed to train before his raging hard-on killed him. If he didn't get some relief soon, Meg's little quip about blue balls wasn't going to be funny at all.

He reached down and covered her hands, at his waist, and squeezed lightly. "We're there."

He felt her shift, her body pressing against his until he swore he could feel her puckered nipples clear through the leather jacket between them, and Mac bit back an oath. He needed space, *now*. Before he did something dangerous and probably stupid. He sensed Meg's head turning and heard her gasp. A wry grin tugged at his lips as he tried to imagine how she must see his hideaway. It was nothing spectacular, by his standards, but Meg's disbelieving sound told him her reaction was quite different.

"What is it?" He asked curiously.

"When you said 'cabin,' I expected a log cabin with the bare essentials," she admitted in an awed murmur. "Mac, this isn't a cabin, it's a *palace!*"

Not hardly. He chuckled at her stunned tone, as he smoothed his hand down her bare thigh. He savored the feel of silky, cool skin beneath his palm and drew in a long, even breath to steady his pulse. Damn, but she felt good. "Not exactly."

Her hands moved, and he winced as her fingertips accidentally brushed over his throbbing cock. How was he supposed to remember the rules when she did stuff like that?

"Are you blind or something?" She sounded incredulous. "It's *huge!*"

He choked off a laugh. Blind? He would be soon if his eyes crossed any further. He couldn't resist a wry, "Thank you, *leannan*. A man likes to know he's appreciated."

She froze, and he winced again, wondering if he'd gone too far. Meg was hard to judge, one moment, she was all sass, and the next, prim and proper. Then, just as he opened his mouth to apologize for his off-color joke, she giggled. *Giggled.* The musical sound burst from her lips and washed over him, sending Mac's libido straight into the stratosphere.

"Not *that!*" She smacked his shoulder lightly, and then shifted against his rear in a motion he had no doubt was calculated. "Though I'd be happy to take a look, if you want my opinion."

His cock twitched with eagerness, and Mac clenched his jaw, an inch from whirling around and giving her exactly what she was asking for. Gods of Light and Shadow, he should have known better! She'd taken his little quip two times around the dance floor and handed it back to him with interest. And damned if he didn't want to take her up on the offer.

"I meant the cabin," she murmured, then he could hear the wicked undertone beneath all that sweetness and innocence.

"Oh." He tried to play along and sound crestfallen, but it was impossible to do with the cool softness of her thigh beneath his hand and the echo of her enchanting laughter still ringing in his ears. He turned to glance at her and grinned warmly. "Aye, it's a pretty big place, I guess. There're fourteen bedrooms, a kitchen, three full baths, a den... all the amenities of home."

The laugh she loosed this time sounded more nervous than delighted. "Your home has fourteen bedrooms?"

"No." He squeezed her thigh as he slid off the bike and turned to grin at her pole-axed expression. She'd best be prepared for a lot more shocks if she intended to go through with this. "My family home has over a hundred rooms."

Her jaw dropped, and her honey-brown eyes grew saucer wide. Mac chuckled. She looked adorable with that stunned expression on her face. "A hundred — ?"

A rueful smile slid over his face. Even among the elite of this world, he figured such a large number would probably be surprising. "My home is a castle, Meg. Remember?"

"Oh, yeah. How could I forget?" Her gaze slid pointedly over his jeans-clad legs and the G80 she still straddled, and one brow lifted skeptically. "You're a regular Prince

Charming."

Even her sarcasm was enchanting. Mac laughed, shaking his head.

"I hope not!" He couldn't help himself, he had to touch her. His hand cupped lightly against her cheek, and he sucked in a breath that smelled of her – warm cinnamon and sweet vanilla, and a shadow scent that was all Meg, and totally enthralling. Great Stars, she had such flawless skin! He'd never encountered its like in this dimension. Touch and scent combined to overload his senses, and desire flared hot and fast, pulling him forward against his better judgment. His voice dropped to a husky murmur as he halted an inch from her delectable lips to whisper, "You, however, are a Goddess among mortals. Sweet Meg…"

Before he could debate the wisdom of his actions, Mac slid his hand to the back of Meg's neck and rubbed lightly as he tipped her head back. Her eyes went wide, the ale-colored depths softened with hunger as her breathing grew swift and shallow. Mac groaned low in his throat, and took possession of her full, sweet lips in a kiss meant to drown all his demons.

*****

Meg gasped softly against Mac's assault as he rocked her mouth open with his hot, commanding kiss. Normally, she didn't like pushy, take-charge men. Meg preferred her lovers to be at least a little malleable. Which didn't explain why every cell in her body electrified whenever Mac got near her. Her nipples peaked, and her breasts strained toward him as he crushed her upper body against his chest. Her skin tingled, and she swore her bones melted on the spot as his clever hands skimmed over her neck and arms. Meg loosed a frustrated moan, needing his hands under her clothes against her bare skin. Oh, yeah, something about Alasdair MacCorran stirred all those secret "bad boy" fantasies she'd told herself were pipe dreams, and sent her libido into overdrive. As he moved to withdraw, she fisted her hands in the smooth, warm silk of his shirt and met the invasion of his tongue with her own bold assault as she returned his kiss with everything she had.

She felt the vibration of his chuckle, and then the groan that followed as he slanted his mouth more firmly over hers, and his hands moved to her hips, their touch no longer gentle. Meg shivered as her sex throbbed with hot need. The cold winter air slipped over her bare thighs and under the hem of her hiked skirt as Mac inched it higher, and the chill sent delicious shivers through her as she melted against him. God, if she didn't know better, she'd swear Mac controlled the very winds, to heighten her pleasure. With a small moan, she rocked her hips against the leather beneath her, and felt Mac's grasp tighten slightly just before he drew away.

"No," she breathed in protest, clutching his shirt tighter. She didn't care if she ripped the damned thing, as long as he stayed put this time, and finished what he started. "Dammit, Mac, I need…"

"Aye, *leannan*. I know," he murmured huskily as he reached up and gently disengaged her hands. "But I can't give it to you."

With that, he scooped her off the G80 and set her on her feet. Meg trembled as her legs readjusted to standing, and then gasped as the ankle-deep snow seeped over the edges of her work sneakers, numbing her toes. The stinging cold brought sanity back in a rush, and mutinous anger along with it. This was rejection number two. A woman could only take so much before she snapped and committed justifiable homicide. As she folded her arms over her chest, Meg felt the bump of the book tucked beneath the jacket she wore and an idea blossomed. There was an entire chapter in that book dedicated to what constituted sex in Mac's world. Heat trickled through her as she considered what possibilities that might leave.

Movement drew her attention, in time to watch a grim-faced Mac stride toward the cabin. Over his shoulder, he instructed, "Follow me. We'll get the interview session out of the way, and then you can rest until we're ready to begin."

Of all the arrogance, as if he ordered her life. Meg followed him silently, glaring at Mac's far-too-appealing backside as she considered murdering him. Rest was the furthest thing from her mind, thanks to that kiss of his, and he damned well knew it. Well, turn about's fair play, she decided with a satisfied smirk. She intended to use her free time to read *Discipulus Optibri* cover to cover, and find out what it took to seduce a sorcerer.

*****

Ten minutes later, Mac sighed as he looked up at the narrow-eyed, angry woman across the table from him, and one of his *seanmhair*'s favorite warnings ran through his head. *Hell hath no fury like a woman scorned…* Never mind that he didn't believe in a Hell. The meaning of that statement was far from lost on him, especially now, facing Meg's hurt rage.

"Full name?"

"Why did you kiss me?" There was sharpness in her tone that cut straight through him. This was bothering her, more than he'd thought it would.

"Because I wanted to," he answered her, simply and honestly. "Your full name?"

Her eyes narrowed to burning amber slits. "What if I didn't want you to?"

He sighed, setting aside the phoenix quill as he looked directly into her fiery eyes. Clearly, they weren't going to get this interview over with until she had an answer that satisfied her. "You did."

She scowled. "Awful sure of yourself."

He let out his breath in an exasperated hiss as he surged to his feet and sidestepped the table to lift her bodily from her seat, depositing her on the tabletop.

"I *am* sure you want me, *siùcar*. You can't

hide it, everything you feel is right here," he murmured silkily, skimming his fingers over her face and watching her eyes widen as her tongue darted over her lips. Spirit of Shadow, she was temptation in the flesh... He leaned in to capture her gaze with his own knowing she could see his hunger in the tiny gasp that left her.

"Your eyes scream sex, *m'calman*, and your breathing grows faint when I do this." It was foolish, but he had to taste her. Leaning in, he put his mouth to the thrumming pulse in her neck, and heard her tiny gasp as she arched toward him, offering him access to that flow of her life source, so trusting, and so responsive. As he skimmed his mouth along the sweet expanse of her throat, Mac trailed his hand over her body, whispering, "Your nipples are hard and," he drew his head back and his eyes closed, his breath hissing out in pleasure, as his hand delved beneath her skirt, cupping against her bare, drenched heat. "You're wet."

"Mac," she moaned as her body arched into his touch, and he couldn't resist slipping one finger into her heat, watching her eyes glaze and close as her head tipped back. She moaned again, her thighs falling open as his finger stroked over her center lightly.

Stabbing heat clenched in Mac's gut, and his entire body throbbed with the want. She was so hot and completely open to him, and all he had to do was unzip his jeans and... and this was totally insane. He *couldn't* have her. With a harsh oath, Mac pulled away, his willpower nearly dying at the husky moan of protest that left Meg.

"You want me," he said again, his voice harsher than he'd intended. Great Shadows, he was steadily going insane with this obsession, and he'd known her less than a day! Stiffly, he moved back around to his side of the table, determined to ignore the shadow-scents of sexual tension. "You want me, and I want you, Meg. But we can't have each other. Rule Number Three, remember?"

She sighed heavily, and muttered something he couldn't hear. "What was that?"

"I said, to hell with your rules, Mac." With that, she slid from the table and dropped angrily into her seat, glaring up at him. "Haven't you *ever* broken a rule? Even bent one a little?"

He kept his gaze on the form in front of him, so she couldn't see how perilously close to breaking the most important rule of magic he really was. "Not the important ones. Your full name, please?"

She sighed again, rolling her eyes. "Megara Lynn Tempest."

Surprise shot through him. That was a unique name, and it stirred a vague memory in him. Had he heard it before? He wasn't sure. "Megara?"

"Yeah." A wry smile quirked on her lush mouth even as her body tensed defensively. Evidently, she'd received enough teasing for her unusual name she'd developed a chip on her shoulder about it.

"It's Greek, supposedly," she explained

with a restless shrug. "My mother named me in honor of my birth country, or what she assumes is my birth country, at any rate."

Mac frowned as he filled her name in on the parchment that would go to the *Illuminata*'s Mistress of Registration. This new piece of information couldn't be good. "You don't know where you were born?"

"Nope." She combed her hands through her dark hair, turning the riot of curls into falls of midnight temptation. Mac swallowed as his eyes followed her motions, noting how her nipples stood out beneath her shirt with every lift of her arms. With effort, he forced his eyes away, wincing at the painful press of metal against flesh in his groin.

"How can that be?" He rasped, surprised at how angry he sounded. Truth was, he needed to get this interview over with, *now*. The soft, shadowy scent of her arousal surrounded him, and he was steadily going crazy with the need to taste her skin.

Meg cast him a curious look, and shrugged. "I was adopted."

He blinked. "Isn't there paperwork?"

"Not for me." She shook her head, causing that glorious hair to ripple over her breasts, outlining the shape of them and nearly bringing him out of his seat in raw lust. "I'm truly a woman without a country. Hell, I barely even have an identity and certainly nothing legal."

"I see." He didn't, really, but he certainly didn't like what he heard. "You're saying you were adopted illegally? Do you have any idea who your birth parents are?"

She snorted a laugh. "Not unless I want to claim a couple of fish in the Aegean, no."

He blinked. "Excuse me?"

"My adoptive parents plucked me out of the Aegean in a basket."

"You're kidding."

"I wish. Believe me, I know how strange it sounds. I didn't believe it myself, at first. Not until Marjory showed me the basket. She kept it, as a souvenir, so she could regale all her hippie friends with tales of how she'd fished poor little me out of the water and raised me as her own, even when I turned out to be a strange, unlucky creature."

Mac winced at the bitterness in her tone. "I take it you and your adoptive parents aren't close."

Meg's answering laugh was sharp. "That's a joke, right? Lee and Marjory Tempest are the original flower children – they believe in free love, free thought, and free drugs. They were on a voyage to 'find' themselves when they found me instead. Not exactly the Cleavers, if you know what I mean."

No, he didn't. He had no idea who these Cleavers were. But from what she said, he got the idea. "Not really, but I think I understand what you're saying."

"The Tempests have more money than brains, and they decided raising a strange baby was a lark, for about four years. Then, they discovered how strange I really was, and suddenly, I wasn't fun any longer. I just cramped their style."

The sadness in her voice brought that odd tightness back to his chest, and he felt his compassion for her rise again. She sounded as if she'd never been loved. So why did he have this sudden impulse to draw her into his arms and just hold her? Why did he feel the need to tell her things he couldn't possibly be feeling? Uncomfortable with the unusual sentiments, Mac pushed them aside and cocked her a questioning look instead. "Strange, how?"

Meg sighed and shrugged awkwardly. "It's really hard to explain, but get me mad enough, and I won't need to. I get pissed enough about something unfair or wrong, and bad things always seem to happen."

Like the power going out at the coffee shop after she'd been fired without even getting a chance to defend her actions. Interesting. Mac rubbed his neck thoughtfully. Apparently, Blackman had made a damned good guess, either that, or he'd been at the receiving end of Meg's rage before. With a wince, Mac knew his money was on the latter. He sighed and ignored the uneasy feeling in the pit of his stomach as he moved on to the next question. "Where did you go to school?"

"You're kidding, right?" She sounded incredulous.

Mac frowned. "Not at all. Some kinds of schools better prepare a person for the discipline required to learn magic than others. What kind of school did you attend?"

She leaned back in her chair and shrugged

as she folded her arms over her chest with a smirk. "The School of Hard Knocks."

Mac's frown deepened at her off-hand reply. She was being flippant, damn it! Didn't she have a clue how serious this was? "Don't be cute, Meg."

"I'm not," she assured him as she rolled her eyes. "I didn't go to school."

He straightened, blinking in disbelief. Meg was bright and clearly educated. How could she have not attended school? "Excuse me? What do you mean, you didn't go to school?"

"I didn't go to school," Meg repeated and then sighed heavily as she leaned forward to rest her forearms on the table between them. "Marjory Tempest is Ms. Free Thought, remember? No daughter of hers is coming within a mile of any traditional school. She and Lee have never liked the idea of being tied down, anyway, and they've got the money to keep moving. They certainly weren't about to let a little thing like my education slow them down.

"I didn't learn from traditional teachers. I learned from experience, and anyone who had a minute to spare for a girl who was hungry for knowledge and human connection. I learned to read from a librarian in Cornwall, and I learned to add and subtract, and keep a checkbook, from an accountant in Milan. I learned to cook from an elderly Philippino grandmother, and to play piano from a retired concert maestro in Prague. I learned from anyone willing to teach, whatever lesson they offered."

Mac rubbed his face in weary disbelief as he listened to her list. He really didn't like the pattern developing here. She had no past, no memories of her birth family, and adoptive parents who'd long ago abandoned self-discipline as boring. Meg had been reared in chaos, and that meant she'd learned little of order or control.

He groaned inwardly, he'd agreed to tutor her in the *Sgàil Ealdhainean*, and he couldn't back out now. But he could see this disaster brewing from a distance. Meg's chaotic early training made her a dangerous element in the world of magic – particularly one requiring the control the *Sgàil Ealdhainean* did. She needed proper magical training from the ground up. However, Mac didn't have time to start at the beginning. *Luna Ascesa* was only a month away. With a muttered oath, he opened his eyes to find Meg's honey-brown gaze fixed solemnly on him.

"What?" He winced at the harshness of his tone and cursed himself as she flinched.

"Are you okay?"

"Aye." He released a breath and flexed his shoulders to release the tension there. Then, with a sigh, he met her gaze again. "What about magic? Do you have any experience?"

She shrugged awkwardly. "I guess I've never really thought about it before. I mean, before today, I probably would have said I didn't even believe it existed."

Mac rubbed his eyes in frustration. Perfect. He had an apprentice, in one of the most difficult fields of learned magic, who didn't even believe in magic. Talk about trying his patience. This wasn't going to be easy, but it wasn't like he had a choice. A bet was a bet, and a deal was a deal.

Resigned, Mac raised his eyes to Meg and stopped, his attention arrested by the sight of her full lower lip scraping between her teeth in a nervous habit. A jolt of pure lust lunged through Mac as his mind painted images of soothing that tormented flesh with his own mouth, sucking away the hurt and laving it with... He snapped his thoughts away from that dangerous direction with a groan as his dick jerked in anticipation. Great Shadows, this woman was temptation in the flesh!

He cleared his throat as he dragged his gaze from her body, before he did something he'd eventually have cause to regret.

"That's enough," he muttered as he rose resolutely.

She smirked, and one dark brow quirked, but it was the vulnerable fear in her eyes that affected him most as she said, "Sounds like you're kicking me out, Mac."

"No. We made a deal," he assured her, but kept his gaze averted, his body angled so she couldn't see the reason why he was so tense. "Come on. I'll show you to your room, and you can get some rest."

Meg hopped to her feet, and he read a restlessness in her motions that mirrored his own. "Why can't we just get started?"

Those words slammed into Mac's strained libido, and he saw all the ways he wanted to "get started." They all involved stripping Meg out of that damned rag of a uniform and tasting every inch of her delectably scented skin. Slapping a lid on those run amok impulses, even as his cock swelled against his fly, Mac offered her a strained smile. She had no idea what she'd just said, looking up at him in total innocence. He'd never had an apprentice so naïve to magic before. Most of the boys who came to him for tutoring were raised in magical families – many in the houses of *Illuminata* or *Sgàil Ealdhainean*.

"*Sgàil Ealdhainean* are easiest done at night when everything is blanketed in shadows. Since you have no formal training in magic —"

She laughed. "You don't have to spare my feelings on the matter, Mac. I have *no* training at all."

"Very well. Since you're untrained, and I don't have time to start with more than the necessary basics of elementary magic, I'll introduce you to the *Sgàil Ealdhainean* when they're easiest to learn." His eyes ran over her coffee-stained uniform, and he grimaced. How could she stand that filthy rag? "In the meantime, you can rest. I'll find you some more appropriate clothing."

Her face flushed, and her eyes glittered with rage and stung pride as she drew herself up tall, her shoulders squared in challenge, and Mac felt a stir of energy on the air. *Uh-oh.* Obviously, he'd just tramped on a sensitive issue.

"What the hell's wrong with the way I look?" She demanded hotly, glaring at him.

Other than she looked like a fantasy come to life – even in that disgusting rag of a garment – and he was finding it impossible to concentrate on anything else? Not a thing.

"You? Nothing," he admitted roughly and then, when her eyes widened in nervous surprise, gentled his tone as he explained, "I just thought you might like some fresh, more comfortable clothing. That uniform looks like you had a very long day."

That was all it took. The air calmed, even as the anger disappeared from Meg's face. No sooner was it gone than Mac wished it'd stayed. Meg was breathtaking in her rage, but that fury also made a man cautious about getting close to her. The soft, vulnerable smile on her lips now, and the grateful light in her eyes, was enough to undo the resolve of even the most determined of men. It was certainly undoing his.

Mac bit back a groan as his body begged to get close to hers, the zipper of his jeans biting into his painful erection. He hadn't lied to her when he said he wanted her. He wanted Meg more than he wanted to breathe. Hell, he didn't care if he never breathed again, as long as it meant the chance to bury himself between Meg's delectable thighs, he knew he'd gladly give up breathing. He winced, and cursed inwardly as the image gelled in his mind and refused to be banished. He couldn't have Meg. And that, he decided with a tortured groan as his eyes slid over her before he turned away, was the worst kind of hell.

*****

Meg followed Mac silently, cursing her rotten luck. She didn't usually pout over men, but, damn it, this one had her so horny her eyes crossed every time he touched her, and still he refused to do anything about it. He kept throwing that damned Rule Three of his at her. Apparently, that rule said he could stick his hands and mouth – but not his dick – anywhere he pleased, as long as she never had an orgasm. Great. Just her luck.

Well, she was a grown woman and she'd deal, Meg told herself with a regal lift of her head. She had the book, after all. She could find out for herself exactly what was and wasn't allowed. She was sure of one thing. Mac's rule might say they couldn't have sex, but she doubted there was any rule that said he couldn't star in her fantasies.

Meg licked her lips, her body tingling as she eyed his muscular ass and thighs, encased in those tight black jeans. She drew a breath and savored the memory of touching him, and of the feel of his rock-hard erection against her hand and body. Drenching heat spiraled through her womb. He wanted to wait until tonight to start her training? Fine by her. She was going to take a nice, long bath and, whether he knew it or not, Alasdair MacCorran was going to give her exactly what she wanted.

## CHAPTER SIX

Only a fool would mess with powers beyond his control. Clearly, the sainted Alasdair MacCorran was more of a fool than he'd imagined, Finnagas Crawford decided as he scowled at the sprawling mountain estate where MacCorran had closed himself away with young Megara. And after that disgusting display he'd seen earlier, Finnagas knew what MacCorran was up to. He was seducing Finnagas' prize, damn it.

The man's scowl deepened as black hatred swept through him. He was Finnagas Crawford, Master *Vanur* of the Crawford clan! He'd spent half a century convincing the *Draoi* he was worthy of the seat of Master *Draoidh*. Even longer convincing the *Illuminata* he deserved the *Rectus Alloquium*, the Right of Address. Then MacCorran had completed his training, and Finnagas had ceased to exist. Alasdair MacCorran was the favored son, the descendant of the *Cheud Draoidh*.

Finnagas' fists clenched in trembling rage. MacCorran had even taken Valentina from him. The woman he wanted, a member of his own clan. She'd wanted him once, too. Then MacCorran had charmed her away, and now all Valentina could talk about was Alasdair, and how she had bedded him, and how she was going to make him her own.

But it was the *Illuminata* Finnagas hated most. Those twelve bitches had denied him his

*Rectus Alloquium*, because of Erinyes Korenes. She'd judged him unfit, and they'd bowed to her will. And he'd sworn revenge. Little Meg's birth had given him exactly what he'd wanted – sweet, blessed revenge. He'd made his move, and still, someone had thwarted him. Damara – a woman of no ability at all – a *mortal*. Somehow, she'd made Meg disappear. He'd thought his chance lost forever. Until last year.

A malicious grin spread over his face. Her power had come into its own, regardless of Damara's pathetic attempts to hide her, and Meg's temper was finally getting the better of her. Last year, the flare of her power had drawn him to Seattle, and he'd followed her ever since, waiting for his chance. Yet, every time he got close, something would happen to make abducting her impossible. His jaw clenched. He'd almost had her this time. She'd been alone at that bus stop. Unprotected, with no one paying attention. Then MacCorran had shown up and whisked her away.

Finnagas' eyes closed, and a plan began to form in his mind. Let MacCorran have his fun – let him fall for Meg, for all Finnagas cared about that. If he could get MacCorran to care about Megara's welfare, he'd have his revenge completely within his grasp – against Erinyes, the *Illuminata*, and MacCorran all in one move. Oh, yes, he decided as he melded back into the shadows, content to watch and wait. Revenge was certainly the sweetest beverage.

*****

Mac paused outside Meg's bedroom door, swallowing hard against the strange tightness in his chest. He felt awkward, something he hadn't felt in decades. Not since he'd been a boy. He wasn't sure how to deal with Meg. When he'd left her at her room door earlier, he'd had to fight the impulse to kiss her. Her anger had been his only saving grace, though he had no idea what she was mad at him about now. She'd been tense – jumpy, really – and she'd disappeared into the room as if some demon was on her tail. He'd heard the click of the lock, and had to smile. He knew that lock was no defense against him, but Meg didn't. She expected the conventions of her world to apply to him.

His gaze dropped to the pile of cloth draping his arms. He didn't know what had made him do it. He could have conjured her up simple, useful clothing at the wave of his hand. He could have altered the shape and make of the clothing she wore, for that matter. But, instead, he'd crossed the *Strata* and talked his mischievous little sister into helping him scour the *Enstrata Forum* for appropriate attire for Meg. Ys had teased him mercilessly, prying for information about Meg, but he'd remained unusually close-mouthed – the first time he'd ever withheld such information from his sister.

Mac swallowed hard. Shopping for Meg hadn't been easy. Picturing her in each and every one of those garments was torture, reminding him of what lay beneath them all. He closed his eyes and bit back an oath. He knew Ys was beyond curious, considering his strange behavior as the trip progressed. But the truth was, he didn't know what was going on either. He wanted Meg. No doubt about that. But there was more. The memory of her vulnerability, and the depth of her honey-brown eyes, punched him in the gut and constricted around his chest.

Mac opened his eyes and stared fearfully at the closed door in front of him. The shopping trip had been nothing. Not compared to the idea of opening this door and confronting Meg in the same space with a bed or, even worse, *in* the bed. His chest tightened with dread. There was only so much a man could take, even a sorcerer.

With a deeply drawn breath, Mac put his hand resolutely on the doorknob and eased the lock open with a flicker of power. He pushed the door open hesitantly, and a weary, relieved breath left him as he saw the room was empty. Then, glancing around, he frowned. The room wasn't just empty. It was undisturbed. How could that be? A shaft of wariness wound through him. He'd come here straight from the *Forum*. Meg should have still been asleep. His frown deepened. Where was she?

A low sound, like a muffled moan, snapped Mac's gaze to the bathroom, and his gut clenched. What on Earth—?

He strode quickly to the door, lifting his hand to the knob, and froze as another of those sounds reached him, and every hair on his body stood on end at the sensual quality of that purring moan. *Spirit of Shadow!* Mac nearly groaned, himself, as he recognized that breathless, throaty sound for what it was, and his mind flashed on images of Meg naked, her hands skimming her own body, arousing herself.

Mac's hand dropped from the doorknob and closed in a trembling fist as he fought the urge to open the door and just watch her. Only, he already knew where that would lead. He'd have to touch her himself, and taste her, and… he was ready to explode, just from the images his mind painted, and the soft sounds of Meg's quickening breath. Great gods, he wanted to be in there with her!

He heard the splash of water, and it nearly brought him to his knees, even before her soft moan reached him.

"Mac."

That single, sultry plea snapped through Mac, and he backpedaled as if burnt. Eyes closed, he drew ragged breaths, fighting the desire to break down the damned door, pull her from her bath and bury himself in her. She wanted him. He'd known that even before now, but knowing she was fantasizing about him while her hands did everything he ached to do was more knowledge than any man should be required to bear.

This was insane. He wanted her too much. How could he want her this much, when he didn't even really know her? Bad enough his cock was so hard he couldn't see straight whenever she was around. However, the tightness in his chest whenever he looked at her, or thought of what she'd told him, was just unacceptable.

With his hands clenched in trembling fists, he turned away from the door, and froze. Blessed spirits! He didn't believe his eyes. He couldn't. If he did, it would mean Meg was capable of things he didn't want to imagine.

Eyes fixed on the bed as his breath grew shallow, he watched a ghostly image of Meg, clothed only in the muted light of the bedroom, slowly stretch out on the sheets with a beckoning smile. He heard the breathless sound of Meg's voice, pleading for his touch, beyond the closed door at his back and his resolve faltered. As impossible as it seemed, Meg could already project herself. And her desire had sent her astral self in search of him. Suddenly, he was glad he was standing in her room, and not in the middle of the *Forum*.

Mac's pulse hammered in his ears, and he was sure his heart was about to break free of its cage in his chest. His eyes never left her as the astral image on the bed tossed her head back, dark hair spilling out on the sheets. She kneaded one breast with a slim hand, her fingers plucking at the nipple, even as the other hand slid down between her splayed thighs, where he could see her arousal in the swollen, glistening folds of her femininity.

Mac swallowed hard, his breath stalled somewhere around his lungs, and the painful pressure of his erection against his fly becoming unbearable. He couldn't even be sure if this was Meg's doing, or his own desire bringing to life images of what he wanted. Not that he cared. Either way, it was a relief. In the arts of magic, he could play as much as he wished, and never cross the line that would damn him. He could have her, and still not actually touch her. It was the perfect solution.

Easing himself onto the window seat, he closed his eyes, unfurled his power completely and reached beyond the bathroom door to Meg.

*****

There was someone in the room with her. That was the first thought to drag Meg up from her fantasy. Mortified embarrassment and fear rushed through her. Regardless that she'd indulged in this form of stress release more than once in the past, it never ceased to embarrass her that someone might find out.

Her eyes flew open, and she stifled a tiny scream as she found Mac bent over her, his bronze eyes as bright as new pennies. Her pulse grew swift, before she stilled, something flickering at the edges of her awareness. There was a strange quality to Mac... or was it *her*? Everything shimmered, and there was a dream-like quality to his form.

"Mac?" She reached out tentatively, unsure what to expect. She was afraid he would disappear at her touch. Her hand met warm silk over hard flesh, and her breath caught. "What're you doing in here?"

He didn't say a word as he lifted her, naked and dripping wet, from the old claw-foot tub. Turning, he set her on the hardwood vanity beside the sink. The cold wood jolted her, but the heat of his hands was distracting. She felt her nipples bead, desperate for his attention. As if he could read her every thought, his hands cupped her aching flesh, moving in gentle circles that were both soothing and erotic, and Meg moaned in frustration. She wanted to beg him to touch her nipples, but she didn't want him to stop what he was doing either.

Her eyes fixed on his, she watched his gaze slide lower, and felt heat prick everywhere his eyes touched. He stepped between her splayed thighs and leaned in. She felt his lips move beside her ear, and his words echoed in her head in a way that made her dizzy with desire. *I'm going to make you come.*

Her eyes widened as those words shot through her, and she sucked in a breath as Mac dipped his head to trace her collarbone in one long lick. Meg loosed a tiny moan, arching forward. "Mac... I thought... We can't..."

He lightly bit her nipple, and then soothed the sting with his tongue, and she bit back a cry, her head falling back as her breasts thrust toward him. She craved him, and she no longer cared if they were breaking the rules. She no longer cared about anything except the need to have Mac inside her. She buried her fingers in his thick, dark hair as she savored the exquisite sensation of his suckling mouth feasting at her breasts. Spirals of heat coiled in her womb, fed by the nipping tug of his teeth and the seductive, rolling lap of his tongue. The tingling in her sex grew into a tight, demanding ache. If he stopped now…

*I'm going to make you come.* The words brushed through her again, in his raspy brogue, and zinged along every nerve. Excitement danced through her, and she quivered with need. She'd been feeling sexy and ready, touching herself while she'd imagined his touch. But no matter how good her imagination was, it couldn't hold a candle to this. Mac's touch was like lit dynamite, it was only a matter of time.

Mac's mouth left her breasts, and Meg moaned in protest, clutching his shoulders as she scooted forward, trying to urge him back to his task. He couldn't stop now!

He chuckled, the sound rushing through her blood like fire.

*What do you want, Meg?* His words whispered along her nerves. *Tell me what you want.*

He was kidding, right? Meg nearly howled with the burning ache in her sex. "I want you to fuck me, dammit!"

He chuckled again, and she was sure she was getting ready to spontaneously combust.

*Such language.*

Like she cared. She gritted her teeth and wrapped her legs around his hips. "Now, Mac."

*Tell me what you want. Do you want me here?* His thumb feathered over her nipple, rolling it slowly beneath the pad as his fingers skimmed her flesh.

God, yes.  Meg arched into his touch, and heard the low hum of Mac's appreciation.  Or was that sound the blood rushing through her own ears?  She shivered, and her sex clenched.  God, Mac had the sexiest voice she'd ever heard, but those noises he made low in his throat were pure sin.

*Are you sure, siùcar?*  His breath trailed along her overheated skin, igniting a brushfire she was sure nothing could extinguish.  Oh, God.  He wasn't...

*Maybe you'd like this better.*  His breath blew warmly against her belly, and Meg's eyes flew open to find Mac kneeling between her splayed thighs.  She gasped, and his eyes lifted to hers, full of raw hunger, before he leaned forward and ran his tongue slowly along the outer slit of her swollen sex.

Meg nearly leapt at the sensation that surged through her at that intimate kiss.  But he didn't give her time to recover.  As she watched through heavy-lidded eyes, he slid his fingers between her nether lips and opened them.  The cooler air against her hot core made Meg gasp, but she barely had time to register that sensation before his mouth latched over the wet flesh, and his tongue moved.  Meg cried out and her hips bucked involuntarily into his ministrations.  Oh, God.  She'd heard about this, before.  She'd just never experienced it herself.

Mac's tongue was killing her slowly as it moved over her in wicked, seductive circles.  Meg stopped thinking completely as she absorbed the sensations.  Her hips arched, and she propped her hands on the countertop and spread her thighs wider as she tossed her head back, moaning, and gave herself over to the sensations Mac was creating.

God, the man's tongue should be bronzed—

The thought flew from her mind as a sensation unlike any she'd ever felt trembled through Meg. Every muscle in her body folded, spasmed, and quivered, and the air stopped in her lungs. Her hips lifted, and a breathless cry tore from her throat as lights exploded behind her eyelids, just before the world went black in the most delicious orgasm she'd ever experienced.

*****

Meg floated back to awareness as a shaft of cold air shivered over her bare skin. Blinking her eyes open, Meg frowned in consternation, and all the amazing sensations evaporated in a wave of uncertainty. She wasn't sure what to believe. Should she believe her sated body and the memory of Mac's touch, which told her he'd just done for her what no man in her life had ever even *thought* of? Or should she accept what her brain and instincts were telling her – that there was something odd about what had just happened?

Meg frowned as she tried to pin down what her instincts were screaming. She was sitting on the edge of the vanity, her legs spread and her body exposed, as if to a lover, no surprise there, except there was no one else in the room. This bathroom wasn't small. How could Mac have disappeared even before she opened her eyes? The door was closed, and she couldn't remember hearing it open or close. She swallowed hard as she realized she couldn't recall it ever opening in the first place.

An uneasy knot formed in her stomach, and she gnawed her lip nervously. Okay, this was getting just a little too weird. Why would she have gotten out of the tub, and hopped up on the vanity, when she'd been just fine in the tub? Yet, she couldn't shake the nagging feeling this hadn't been as real as it seemed.

Her memory flashed over the dream-like quality of Mac, and she sat bolt upright as she recalled that, while she'd swear she'd felt his breath and touch on her body, she couldn't remember actually *hearing* the words he'd said. They'd been whispered in her mind. She groaned, slumping back against the wall, her eyes closed. Great. There was no way she'd imagined what had happened, but she couldn't prove she *hadn't*, either. Maybe she was just going nuts. Yeah. She was turning into a regular Sybil.

A soft knock on the bathroom door startled her, and Meg jumped, her heart pounding as her eyes flew open. Fear stumbled through her. She had no idea what was going on around this place, but there was no way she was opening that door until she knew who, or what, was on the other side.

"Meg?"

A pulse of heat shot through her blood at that husky brogue, but was chased away by the icy realization that Mac was on the other side of the bathroom door. And he'd *knocked*! Why would he do that, if he'd just been in here, making her crazy with his tongue?

"Y-yes?" She managed in a shaky voice as she fought back a wave of disappointment and fear. She'd never had such a vivid experience in her life, it was a letdown to know it was probably just her imagination working overtime. She shifted, another jolt of uneasiness going through her. It'd been *too* vivid, even for her imagination. She'd never experienced that kind of intensity before.

"Are you okay?"

Oh, God. Meg slid to the floor on trembling, unsteady legs as her stomach lurched. Had she screamed when she came? She couldn't remember. God, what if she'd cried out his name? Heart pounding as she scrambled to come up with a reason she'd be crying out his name without giving away what she'd been doing, she distractedly pulled open the door. She drew a breath, and released it. She'd play innocent, if he asked.

"I'm fine," she assured him quietly.

There was a moment of complete silence, and then a soft oath, and she lifted her gaze to his with a puzzled frown. His bronze eyes were brighter than she remembered, reminding her of when he'd bent over her naked body, and her skin tingled as… She gasped, straightening, as she realized she was standing before him completely nude, her skin still damp, and flushed with the afterglow of sexual release.

Mortified heat shot through her, just before she watched amusement thread into the heat in his gaze, and her embarrassment turned to white-hot rage.   How *dare* he laugh at her! Defensively, she snatched a towel from the shelf near the door and wrapped it around her.  Her cheeks burned with anger as she snapped, "What do you want?"

His eyes stayed focused on her chest for a long moment, before all signs of amusement dropped from his eyes, and he abruptly turned away.   "I left some clothes on your bed.  Get dressed.  We begin lessons in one hour."

With that, he stalked across the bedroom and disappeared through the door.  Meg stared at the door as it slammed behind him, confused by his sudden brusqueness.  Okay, *she* wasn't going nuts.  This place was brimming over with what her mother would call "loony vibes."

Hurt and anger mingled in Meg as she roughly toweled off.  What did Mac think she was, a toy?  He'd had his hands all over her since Seattle, driving her crazy with want, and yet he seemed to think she shouldn't get itchy for sex.  He'd just seen her without a stitch of clothing on, and she still had yet to even see him without his *shirt*.  She wasn't too proud to admit she wanted to.  She was desperate to.  Meg licked her lips as she wondered if his chest was smooth or hairy, and if his body was every bit as muscular as it felt beneath that silk shirt and jeans.  Her hands itched to find out.

Meg groaned as she felt the flush of desire stir again. God, she had it bad. She was in perpetual lust here, lust that would only be sated when Mac finally finished what he started.

Stepping into the bedroom, Meg saw the small pile of colored cloth and crossed to it, curious, in spite of herself. Mac said he'd bought her some clothes. Normally, even the idea would have infuriated her. She was a big girl, after all, and quite capable of buying her own clothes. She could thank Marjory for that one thing. As dippy as she usually was, Marjory Tempest was a feminist to the core, and she'd instilled a sense of independence in her daughter that more than one man had found intimidating. But not Mac.

A strange, warm feeling crept through Meg as she reached out to stroke a finger over one charcoal-gray patch of material. Mac had shopped for her, though he didn't seem the type who'd be comfortable with the task. And, she was grateful enough to not be wearing that disgusting uniform any longer that, she was pleased, Mac was thoughtful enough to get her new clothes. She wasn't going to look a gift horse in the mouth, at any rate.

Meg sorted through the small pile of clothes, and her throat tightened with every item she uncovered. They were beautiful! Garments of air-light silk and breezy cotton, in deep, vibrant shades ranging from a golden yellow to deep, twilight purple and dusky gray. Lifting one light fall of royal blue from the pile, she gasped as she shook out an amazing, knee-length dress with poet sleeves and a sweetheart neckline, and fell in love. It was the most awesome garment she'd ever seen! As she blinked away tears, she noticed something else. A smooth, satiny strap.

Curious, she reached to flip aside a forest-green skirt, and a small laugh bubbled up through her tight throat as she took in the rainbow of sheer, skimpy lingerie. Panties and bras, stockings, and she didn't even want to hazard a guess at what a few of the other items were she decided as a blush crept up her neck. Clearly, Mac intended for her to be *fully* clothed in his presence. Her heart skittered as she remembered the heat in his eyes, and wondered if he was as tempted as she. It was damned hard to tell through that control he was remarkably adept at. A wicked smile curved on her lips. If he was as desperate as she was, maybe…

With a sharply indrawn breath, Meg pushed the thought, and the heat it stirred, away. She wasn't going to think about Mac and sex. That was a sure way to repeat her confusion, and she still hadn't made any sense of it. Quickly, she donned matching blue bra and panties, shifting uncomfortably at the confined feeling, but liking the way the underwire bra pushed her breasts up, giving her C-cup a little more lift. No wonder other women swore by this stuff. It did amazing things for her figure, not to mention her confidence. She grinned as she realized Mac might have made a tactical error in providing her with the undergarments.

She eyed the daunting pile of silk stockings and strips of satiny elastic, and decided she didn't know how to put the damned things on, or even what those strips *were*, aside from what appeared to be some kind of belt. She wasn't going to ask Mac, either. Likely, he'd show her, and she'd have to endure his touch again. With his repeated rejections, and the disturbing fantasy she'd had, the idea of his hands on her body stirred an uncomfortable, restless feeling she didn't want to examine too closely. Nope. She'd forgo stockings. Thanks to the ridiculously short skirts Phil the Pill required his waitresses to wear, Meg shaved and moisturized her legs every day, so she wouldn't need stockings. Odd, how she was grateful of that now. Meg laughed quietly, and shook her head.

She slipped the royal blue dress over her head, and sighed with pleasure at the feel of cool, smooth silk sliding along her skin. The dress was positively sinful, falling to just above her knees in soft waves of material that felt like water spilling over her. As she finger-combed her damp hair into a riot of curls and left the room, she wondered if she'd pass muster with Mac, now. Clearly, her uniformed work self hadn't.

*****

Mac heard the shuffle of movement from upstairs, followed by the soft sound of a door being closed, and more shuffling. The first creak of the stairs sent his blood rushing as he tensed.

He itched to turn, and go to the bottom of the stairs. He wanted to see which of his offerings she'd chosen. Not that any of them would do that heavenly body justice. He swallowed hard, dragging in a breath as his dick twitched and swelled again. Gods and demons, this was insane! He'd finally got his body under control and, with one sound, Meg Tempest took over again.

Schooling himself to cold indifference, he turned toward the stairs as Meg descended into view, and promptly felt the ground fall out beneath his feet. His breath stalled, and his jeans bit into his erection as indifference flew away. Great Shadows!

The woman who descended his stairs bore little resemblance to the harried, unkempt waitress he'd so easily dismissed back at the coffee shop. Her dark hair, which had defied taming then, now hung freely around her, spilling over her shoulders and down her back in a curly riot that made her look fresh out of bed, and sexy as sin. Mac nearly swallowed his tongue at the memory and shadow images that thought stirred, even as his gaze slid lower, and his gut clenched in desire. She'd picked the blue dress!

Mac had known, the moment he saw it hanging in a Gypsy's stall, only one woman in all the *Strata* could ever wear that dress. The old woman had confirmed his thought, and he'd known only Meg could do the dress justice. He just hadn't known how much, until now.

The royal blue of the silk rested against her

light, olive-toned skin as if it'd been crafted solely for her. That deep, vibrant color brought out the tone of her flawless skin, and showcased those luminous honey-brown eyes, making them seem even larger and more mysterious than before. Starlight lines of silk shimmered as they hugged the amazing curves Meg's frumpy uniform had been designed to hide, and the neckline of the dress dipped sensuously between her breasts, demure, and yet displaying an expanse of skin that made his mouth water. The skirt ended above her knees, and showed off less of her legs than the uniform had. But it flirted around those smooth-skinned thighs in a way that left him breathless.

His gaze slid over her shapely calves, and stopped on her bare feet, and an involuntary smile tugged at Mac's lips. Encased in silk, Meg looked sophisticated and sensuous. Confident. But those bare feet, even after the assortment of shoes he'd procured, were the simple, unvarnished essence of Meg. Wild, free, and yet vulnerable in ways that tugged at his heart, surprising him.

Lifting his gaze to hers, he smiled softly. "You look beautiful."

A shy smile flicked at her lips, and the vulnerable uncertainty in her eyes punched Mac square in the gut with his mistake. Meg used her powers unconsciously, and in total innocence. In his need for her, he'd managed to forget she was new to his world. She didn't understand the *Sgàil Ealdhainean*, or how it could be used. Now, thanks to his slip, she was embarrassed, and afraid he'd overheard an intimate fantasy, instead of accepting him as a participant of an event that had blown them both away.

He owed her better. After all, she'd trusted him enough to come here. Determined to put her at ease, he offered her another smile as he turned toward the patio door. "As gorgeous as you look in that, *mil*, a coat might be in order."

She took the last few stairs in a graceless clatter. "You're kidding! Mac, it's got to be below freezing out there by now!"

He shot her an amused glance. "Aye. That's why I suggested a coat." His gaze dropped to her feet, and his smile widened. "Shoes, too."

"If you think I'm going out in the freezing cold in this dress, you're insane." She issued that proclamation in a disgusted mutter as she flounced back up the stairs. Mac bit back his laughter as he watched her go. Aye, Meg had a spirit unlike any he'd ever seen. She had a quick temper, but a regal sense of command that would do any *Illuminata* proud. His gaze dropped to her rear, moving sleekly beneath shimmering silk, and he had to suck in a deep breath as she disappeared from view. He heard a door slam. Meg was off-limits, no matter what they'd done earlier. No matter what that silk made him think of doing now.

*****

Moments later, Meg was back, and Mac

immediately regretted choosing to do her training outside. The silk dress was gone, exchanged for a pair of heavy, loose jeans and a bulky sweater – items he'd seen as necessities of survival for Meg, and spurred by that annoying protective instinct of his. A heavy, fleece-lined coat was draped over her arm, and hiking boots adorned her feet. Suddenly, mysterious, seductive Meg was gone, replaced by Ms. All-American. She looked fresh, clean, wholesome, and… *young*. It struck Mac, suddenly. She bore a striking resemblance to someone. Something in the tilt of her chin, and the forthright light shining in those ale-colored eyes nagged him. And why had he never thought to ask her age?

"How old are you?"

Her lips quirked. "Wondering if you've been making passes that'll land you in jail?"

He frowned. "Without the sarcasm."

She tilted her head to the side, and that sense of *deja vù* was back. "Old enough to know better than to answer that question."

"Meg…"

"I'm twenty-five, best I can tell without a birthday, okay?" She rolled her eyes as he frowned. "Sheesh. I told you, I don't know anything about my past, for sure. What difference does a year or two make?"

Mac blinked, surprised. Most people preferred to at least *know* when they were born. If Meg was right, she was about a decade younger than him, and she didn't seem the least bit interested in knowing where she'd come from. How could a grown woman not even be curious? And why did she look so damned familiar?

"Absolutely none," he finally answered her. He'd save the discussion about her lack of interest in her own past for another time. They had work to do right now. He gestured toward the snow-covered patio. "Shall we?"

She flashed him a nervous smile. "If you insist. But don't say I didn't warn you this is a mistake."

In more ways than one, Mac conceded as he watched her stride toward the door. Every sense he possessed told him Meg was trouble with a capital "T." He only hoped she could be trained to control what she did as naturally as breathing, or their troubles might just be starting.

## CHAPTER SEVEN

Finnagas watched through narrowed eyes as Meg left the mansion's back door, MacCorran on her heels. He'd sensed the spike of power earlier, and knew something had happened. He'd thought about using his *Vanur* abilities to get into the house, but quickly discarded it as useless. Alasdair MacCorran might make himself a fool over a woman, but he was too aware of the dangers of this backward dimension to leave his home wide open. There had to be some kind of power shields on the place, MacCorran was tricky enough to have hidden them from prying eyes.

He kept his eyes glued on the couple as MacCorran gestured, as if he was explaining something to Meg. They were too far away to hear what was said, but he could see Meg's nod, and the uneasiness that crept over her face. With a wave of his hand above the snow-covered ground, MacCorran cleared a space on the ground, and Finnagas scowled. Show-off. Even from here, he could see Meg was impressed though MacCorran seemed to not even notice. MacCorran gestured again, and Meg cast him a wary glace before settling herself cross-legged on the ground. MacCorran smiled reassuringly, and waved a hand in front of the woman's face, obscuring her eyes with a dark shadow before he stepped back and said something to her. Finnagas gritted his teeth. He could only guess what MacCorran was up to, but if it involved Meg, it might just provide the distraction he needed to get her away.

*****

What was she *doing* here? Meg's heart beat harshly in her ears as she sat where Mac instructed. A thick, dark blindfold of some kind covered her face, and she shifted nervously, feeling the edges of panic creeping in around her. It wasn't that she worried about Mac doing anything improper – hell, she wished he *would*. At least then she wouldn't be feeling so...*twitchy*. And that wasn't a good feeling either. There were eyes on her, she could feel them. Eyes that meant her harm. Eyes she'd been feeling for the past year without fail. Meg shifted uncomfortably.

"Sit still," Mac instructed.

She tried. Oh, God, she was trying to do exactly what he told her, what he'd explained in detail. She tried to focus on letting the excess energy flow from her body into the ground, as he'd showed her. But she couldn't. Not with this damned blindfold on! Meg bit the inside of her cheek against screaming in anger and fear. She needed to see, dammit!

It wasn't that she had anything against blindfolds. In the proper setting, they could be quite sexy. And she certainly wasn't claustrophobic. She'd spent the first eight years of her life in a houseboat barely bigger than a saltbox. However, sitting out here in the open, she had the distinct feeling she was in danger, and she needed to *see* that danger! She couldn't spot trouble, couldn't defend herself, if she couldn't see. Not that she knew why that should matter, but it did. Deeply.

"Mac…" She pleaded in a whisper.

"Shh. Concentrate," he admonished sternly, all trace of the man who'd set her libido into orbit wiped away. He sounded more like a drill sergeant than a tutor or a lover.

Anger rose along with her panic, and she clawed at the blindfold, unable to find the purchase to rip it free. "Dammit, Mac! I can't concentrate with this blindfold on!"

"You need to learn to see without your eyes," he explained in a tone that bordered on impatience. "Concentrate on the feel of the energy as it flows through you, and direct that flow toward where you want it to go. Push it toward the ground."

"I can't."

"You *can*."

Meg's anger and panic boiled into frustrated rage, even as the claustrophobia– what else could she call it – closed in. "Are you deaf? I said I *can't!*"

*****

Mac's eyes widened at the wave of furious energy that hit him as the ground beneath his feet trembled and buckled. His eyes widened in disbelief as the rolling, trembling sensation continued to grow, even after Meg's anger subsided. It felt as if the earth beneath them had run mad. Wings fluttered in the surrounding forest as the birds abandoned their winter nests, taking to the sky as they would for an earthquake. Mac's head snapped around as a rattling began, and he watched heavy wooden lawn furniture dance across the stone deck. Blessed Shadows, this was no earthquake!

His eyes went back to Meg as wary fear crossed the surface of his mind. Just who, and *what*, was this woman? After what had happened back at *Hole in the Wall*, he *knew* this was Meg's doing. But what had prompted it? Somehow, he didn't think the blindfold affected her much. Her face was flushed with frustrated, frightened heat, and her hands were fisted in her lap until he was sure her nails were cutting grooves into her palms. She was clearly trying to do as he'd asked, even though she admitted she couldn't concentrate. He swallowed as he watched her. What power did this woman possess that the earth itself trembled whenever she tried to ground?

"Meg, stop!" He ordered, unable to keep a little of the fear roiling inside of him from his voice. If he didn't stop her now, she could break the world apart with her energy. With a flick of his hand, he waved the shadowy blindfold away as he hurried toward her.

Her eyes blinked open, and she stared up at him with owlish, unfocused eyes for a long moment, before she crumpled to the snowy ground, her eyes fluttering closed. Mac dropped to his knees, yanking her into his arms and shaking her lightly as concern tugged at him. She was too still…

"Meg," he called softly, slapping her face gently. "Meg, wake up!"

She moaned, shifting in his arms, and the open vulnerability of her face was more than he could stand. His chest tightened to aching, and a lump he couldn't seem to swallow lodged in his throat. Leaning over her, he placed soft, soothing kisses on her forehead.

"Meg, *leannan*, open your eyes," he murmured as he shook her again. Fear plunged through him. She was in danger. He knew too well the effects of an involuntary ground. She had to open her eyes, or she risked succumbing to the drain of her vital energies.

Her eyes opened slowly, and the wild pain and fear there punched Mac hard in the gut. Great Stars! She looked like she was already dying!

"Mac." Her voice was faint with fear and pain, as if she couldn't draw a complete breath, and the word was a whispered plea across his mind.

He drew a deep, steadying breath as he realized what was happening. Meg wasn't just draining her power supply, she had tapped into her life-source in her effort to ground. She fed off the elemental energy that sustained her life, and she was draining it straight into the ground. His pulse skipped a beat in dread. He had to stop this! He had to stop her before she drained herself completely. But the only way to stop an involuntary ground of life-force energy was to redirect the energy flow and, as his gaze fell on her lips, his scrambling mind could only latch onto one solution. A solution that broke every rule Mac knew he couldn't break.

He didn't have a choice. With a small groan of resignation, he leaned over her and sealed his lips to Meg's, drawing her energy into himself and feeding it back to her in a steady stream. His heart hammered, and he could feel the rapid flutter of Meg's pulse as it twined with his own in a wave of fiery energy the likes of which he'd never experienced before. It was electric, this awareness, a blending of shadow and light that left him dizzy with need.

Meg's arousal clawed through his awareness as it took over, and he knew everywhere she ached for his touch. His body reacted predictably, and he knew she could feel his need as well as her hand slipped over the erection straining against the fly of his jeans. With a growl of need, he plunged his hands beneath her jacket and up, shaping them around her breasts as his thumbs ran in circles across her hard nipples.

Meg arched into his touch as she broke their kiss with a cry, and something suddenly impacted Mac like a lightning bolt, sending him sprawling backward across the patio. He crashed into a wrought-iron bench and lay there, stunned, as he watched the air around Meg shimmer, before her eyes opened, and she blinked, disoriented. "Wha... Mac, what happened?"

A grim smile tugged at Mac, though he didn't feel like smiling, as he rose to his feet, rubbing his head. "What happened, *m'suiteas*, is a warning of what's going to happen from now on whenever we attempt to break the rules."

She met his eyes, and he read uncertainty in those honey-brown depths before she licked her lips nervously. "But… We've kissed before, and it hasn't…"

"Not like that," he whispered, closing his eyes. Great Shadows, he could still feel her in his blood. Mac groaned, realizing the truth of his words. Whether intentionally or not, they'd broken the very rule he'd hoped to avoid by denying the sexual tension between them. They'd broken the most important rule of magical training.

Because of the nature of magic, two *Magi* of the same power level who engaged in sex risked blending their powers and consciousnesses. While, in two properly trained and aware *Magi*, this was normally considered a fortuitous event, the union between one of high power that was still untrained and unbalanced, and one of trained ability, could lead to disaster. And if he was right about Meg being *Illuminata*, he was in even bigger trouble now.

They hadn't had sex. Unfortunately, that was no defense, since it didn't take sexual union to break the rule of blending powers. By rights, from the first moment he'd kissed her, back in Seattle, he'd crossed a line he couldn't take back. And, with her life-source exposed when they kissed just now, they'd risked the same blending that came with sex. And the unthinkable had happened, that one kiss had bound them together.

Mac swallowed hard. He had no idea how they'd managed to meld powers, because one taste of her source told him Meg could never practice *Sgàil Ealdhainean,* not the way a *Draoidh* did. Her abilities were duality-based. She was a Judge's apprentice, not a *Draoidh's.* Still, they'd made a deal, and he couldn't break that pact without disgracing himself and his family. Now, with his power mated to hers, the magic of the *Sgàil Ealdhainean* flowed in her veins as it did in his. This could be a *big* problem. Meg's nature to Judge could cause absolute disaster with access to a volatile magic like the *Sgàil Ealdhainean.* And, if it did, the world could pay for that mistake.

# CHAPTER EIGHT

Meg groaned as she pulled one of the king-sized bed's pillows over her head and fought the urge to scream. She wanted to *sleep*, dammit! She wanted to sink into total oblivion and never show her face again. What she didn't want to do was replay that entire moment of stupidity again. God, what must Mac think of her?

She'd kissed him. Not some piddling little kiss, or even one of those body-clenching liplocks they'd shared before. She'd *kissed* him, heart and soul. She'd poured everything she was into that kiss. He had to know now. He might have suspected she'd been touching herself, earlier, he might have even had an idea she'd been fantasizing about him. Now, he wouldn't have to guess or wonder. She didn't question why she was aware of that, she only knew she was. Embarrassingly so.

Meg yanked the pillow from her face and stared at the ceiling morosely. God, how had she screwed up so bad? Mac made magic look *easy*. He exuded total confidence and competence, and he instinctively did things she'd never even seen done before. So she'd convinced herself *she* could do the same things. Then she'd gone and made a disaster of it all. Typical Meg. Her expression turned sour with self-disgust.

She heaved a sigh of disgust, swung her legs out of bed and sat up. She yanked on her robe against the slight chill of the night-draped cabin and rose from the bed. She wasn't going to sleep tonight. The least she could do was try to drown out her troubling thoughts with the one thing that always soothed her– music.

*****

Mac prowled restlessly from the window to the door, and back, battling temptation with every step. As he stopped at the door, hand on the knob, for the tenth time in the past fifteen minutes, Mac pressed his forehead against the cool wood with a tortured groan, his free hand clenched in a shaking fist. He wanted to storm down the hall to Meg's room and claim her with all the raw lust that still tangled in his gut. Instinctively, he knew she'd meet his savage passion with her own – they were equally matched in that dark realm not even the elusive *Sgàil Ealdhainean* could touch.

His jaw clenched as his body throbbed with the lust he couldn't banish. Spirits of Shadow, he could *still* taste her on his lips, still smell the sweet nectar of her desire. Meg filled up every pore of his body until he wanted to rage with the painful need she stirred. But he wouldn't. He was a Master *Draoidh*, damn it all, he *would* control himself!

Mac's raised his head as, through the hot blood pulsing in his ears, he heard the faint strains of a familiar tune. He froze. Music? How could that be? No one played the baby grand piano Ys had begged him to put in the cabin's unused formal dining room four years ago. He knew his sister had plans to play the instrument, someday, she would learn music as well as song and Weaver Magic at Bardic school. And she had a natural ear for music. But Ysabet wasn't here. She wouldn't cross the *Strata* alone at night.

Brows furrowed in concern, Mac eased open his door and cautiously made his way down the stairs. At the entrance to the formal dining room, he stopped, feeling as if someone had sucked every drop of air from his body, leaving him weak and dizzy – with need.

Meg, bathed in the pale light of the half-moon that shimmered through the window behind her like Faery dust, was seated at the piano. Her head was tipped forward until curtains of midnight curls concealed her features, yet he knew, from the motions of her body, her eyes were closed and her entire being was bound up in the soft, haunting sounds she drew from the baby grand. Her slim fingers drifted over the keys, the notes sure but unhurried, as her body swayed lightly. She was, he realized with a small gasp, using Weaver Magic without conscious awareness. She was weaving a spell that held him totally enthralled.

He moved up behind her and froze as his eyes fell on the back of her neck. Meg's parted hair revealed the long column of her neck, and there, right at the base of her hairline, was a mark every child of the *Lux Magica* was taught from birth to recognize on sight. A bright white patch of skin – made more apparent by Meg's olive complexion – in the shape of a tipped-up crescent moon, glared up at him in the pale moonlight. There could be no doubt now. Meg was *Illuminata*.

Mac sucked in a sharp breath as he realized how much trouble he was in. Meg's shoulders tensed at the sound, and her head snapped upright.

"Mac?" Her query was tremulous as she sat frozen, her gaze fixed straight ahead. "What do you want?"

He reached out and threaded his fingers lightly through her hair, his eyes closed at the subtle fragrance that lifted from the ebony strands. Spirits of Shadow, she smelled amazing.

"Mac?" Her query emerged a soft whisper as she shivered lightly and arched into his touch.

"All I want," he murmured as he scooped her hair away from her neck and bent to press his lips to the birthmark on her otherwise flawless skin, "is you."

A soft moan broke Meg's lips as her head tipped forward again, exposing her neck in invitation. Mac drew a shuddering breath, fighting the desire that hummed in him. His body begged him to take what she offered and sate the hunger that raged in his blood. His brain knew better. Not only was Meg his apprentice, and therefore untouchable by the rules of magical mentorship, but she was *Illuminata*, and no one got more untouchable for him than that.

With an oath, he paced away from her and drew in deep breaths of night air in an attempt to clear the tantalizing scent of her from his lust-hazed mind. He stopped at the window, staring out at the blanket of fresh snowfall. A sharp laugh broke his lips. "This is insane."

A heavy sigh answered him before she said, "I couldn't agree more. Look, we both want it, and I'm not getting anywhere with the magic lessons. How about we just forget the apprenticeship?"

That was a disaster in the making for them both. Mac winced and shook his head sharply. "No."

"Why not? The training's been a waste of both our times…"

He rubbed his face wearily and fought the urge to swear again. It must be nice to be so oblivious. Unfortunately, *he* wasn't. He knew that even dissolving the apprenticeship wouldn't make sex between them any more allowed. Besides, he couldn't dissolve the apprenticeship, and he couldn't tell Meg why not. He couldn't tell her about the bet, or he'd lose any chance he might have of ever being worthy of her. For reasons he didn't fully understand, he knew he couldn't risk that. "I can't tell you why not, but it's not an option. Just suffice to say we can't quit your training now."

"Fine." Her voice was stiff and flat, her shoulders braced against pain, and she began setting her fingers slowly and deliberately over the keyboard.  "So what do you propose we do?"

He could hear the pain and disappointment in her voice, and it struck him hard.  He wished he could give her everything she wanted.  But he couldn't, and that was that.  His hands clenched as he muttered, "I wish I knew."

## CHAPTER NINE

They'd been at this for over a week, and they were still working on basics. Maybe Meg was right, after all, maybe this *was* pointless. Mac sighed to himself as his gaze glued to the gentle sway of Meg's sweet ass as she strode toward the trees on the far side of the garden. In a week, all he'd accomplished was to put himself in a state of constant, painful arousal. It was disconcerting, to feel his control slipping so badly.

He'd never wanted a woman so much he couldn't control his impulses before. But, ever since she had looked up at him with those wide, honey-brown eyes, he'd been unable to banish fantasies of Meg, naked and in his arms. Now, thanks to the melding of their energies in the kiss they'd shared last week, the constant hum of awareness was driving him crazy. He needed to have her, to prove to himself that reality wasn't nearly as potent as the fantasies his fevered mind stirred.

Mac rubbed his face and sighed. It wasn't that they weren't making progress. Meg had actually managed to ground herself without a disaster yesterday. But it'd taken way too long to get to this point. The training was taking too much time, they should have been past this point a week ago.

Not that he was complaining. Meg's mastery of grounding provided a temporary alleviation of the tension radiating between them. Mac groaned as his eyes slid over Meg, and his fly grew painfully tight. If only they could figure out a way to douse the flames *permanently*.

"Mac?" The light, soft sound of her voice drifted to him on the winter air, pulling his attention back. Night was falling fast, and even from where he was standing, he could see the glow of her eyes – the constant reminder of why he couldn't ever have what he wanted, because all he wanted was Meg.

"Now what do I do, Mac?"

He drew a breath of cold air and focused his entire attention on his job as mentor. He had to stay focused on Ys, and everything that was riding on what they accomplished here, or he had no doubt he'd give in to temptation, eventually.

"Gather your power like I showed you earlier," he instructed as he moved to stand a short distance away. "Let it build until you can feel the shadows all around you, like a living, breathing cloak. You command it with your mind and your power – the shadows of every world respect only those who feel no fear in their folds. When you can feel the shadows growing without fear, reach out with your mind and pull the cloak of it around you, like so."

Mac drew in his power, formed the growing shadow around his hand, and waved it across his face, letting the shadow wash over him until his entire body was engulfed.

"Mac? Mac!" He heard her frantic cry, and saw her tense, her gaze moving wildly. He waved the shadow away and saw her visibly relax. "Dammit, Mac, don't *do* that!"

He chuckled. Any third-year student of Elementary Magic would have known what he'd done and been unfazed by the simple disappearing trick. He was absurdly glad Meg was surprised – he liked the idea of being able to get close to her without her awareness. Unbidden, the image of moving within the shadows of her room, while she slept, leapt to his mind. He could watch her, touch her, even make love to her and she would believe it all a dream. Mac frowned. He didn't want her to think of their union, when it finally came, as a dream. He already hated that their little shadow dance in her bathroom was something she viewed as a sexual fantasy… and he was letting himself get distracted again.

"You try it," he urged her gruffly, and saw her eyebrows rise at his tone. "Go on. Try it."

He watched her draw a deep breath, and felt her power stir and draw together, until he could feel the prickle of hair standing on end even as the crackle of unseen energy sparked flickering lights… Mac swore beneath his breath as he realized what she was doing. "Meg! *Stop!*"

She froze, and Mac felt the curl of her power feeding back into itself, like a closed circuit. Horror rushed through him. She could perform a Flare Ring without thought or training. Blessed Spirit of Shadow! He had to stop her, before… He felt the ring of power spiral through the air, like an invisible beam.

"*No!* Damn it, Meg, don't release the power! Don't—"

An explosion of sparks lit up the descending night, like fireworks at ground level. The trees around Meg burst into flame and he heard Meg's frightened scream, felt it pierce him to his source. She couldn't protect herself!

"*Lasair a mach!*" Mac flung his hand, fingers splayed as if to catch the showering sparks and licking flames, and a shadow so dark no light could penetrate it descended over the area, the chill of it dousing the flames completely.

As the shadow receded, Mac felt his thundering pulse hammer in his head, his heart racing with adrenaline fed by fear.

"Meg!" He rushed to where she huddled, trembling, amongst the charred remains of the grove.

"Shh." He crouched beside her and pulled her gently from her locked posture and into his embrace. She wasn't crying, yet. The shock hadn't worn off, she was still in the grip of the power she'd released.

Mac rocked her gently as her body trembled uncontrollably, and his heart cracked wide as the first sob tore from her. Damn it, he'd known she was at the end of her rope, physically, mentally, and emotionally, Meg was exhausted. This was *his* fault, his arrogance and fear. He'd pushed her too hard, to prove to himself he was in control. And for what? Meg's rapport with her magic was too fragile to stand up under the constant strain of being directed on a Path that was clearly not her first nature. Remorse jabbed him like a blade.

"Why can't I do what you do?" Meg railed in frustrated sobs as Mac hugged her closer and cursed himself as an arrogant fool for ignoring her fragile sense of self-worth. He'd been so busy pressing that prickly exterior of hers, he'd completely overlooked the uncertainty it hid.

"This isn't your fault, *leannan*," he murmured as he brushed his lips over her dark curls. "It's mine. I keep forgetting you can't learn to do this the same way I did."

She pulled away a little, and the confusion in her luminous, ale-colored eyes punched Mac in the chest, nearly rocking him back on his heels. The sensation surprised him. It'd been too long since he'd cared how his words affected anyone.

"So what can we do?" Her query was soft and sad with defeat.

"I'm not sure," he admitted gently, cupping his hand against her neck, unable to resist the urge to touch her no matter how wrong it was. "But we'll figure something out."

And, as her beautiful eyes overflowed with gratitude, the knot of need in Mac's gut pulled tight, shattering even the illusion of control. He no longer questioned his intentions, or even his right. He simply followed his instincts and bent his head, slanted his mouth over hers, and drank in every ounce of sweetness he could.

*****

Meg's heart stuttered and then stalled completely, as Mac's hot, hungry kiss rocked through her. She felt raw, and needy, and she didn't care what Mac's rulebook said. She wanted him to take her away from all this frustration and failure, she wanted him to let her hide herself in the one thing she *knew*, in her soul, would be right – sex with Mac.

Her hands arrowed beneath his leather jacket and smoothed over his shirt – more of that silky material, this time in a deep burgundy that made his features even more startling to her overcharged system – even as she felt his hands meld to her hips, moving in restless circles as he drew her deeper into his embrace. She could feel the shadowy presence of him and the closing darkness of night. Amazingly, for a girl who'd once lived in terror of the shadows, the surrounding darkness no longer frightened her. In Mac's arms, she felt safe and cherished. Nothing that haunted the shadows of her memory could harm her, as long as he held her. She didn't have to be strong, alert, or wary. She only had to *feel*. It was a liberating experience.

His hands skimmed her breasts, and Meg moaned as that light brush, even through the layers of her clothes, made her skin tingle. What Mac did to her was magic, and—

Meg sucked in a sharp breath as she jerked away from Mac. *Magic.* That was it, that was all this was about. He was testing her resolve, her ability to abide by the rules he'd set down.

She'd watched his iron-hard control at work when he'd effortlessly shown her the wonders of magic. He wouldn't bend or break the rules without a good reason.

"What?" His voice *sounded* raw enough. Doubt plunged through Meg. She licked her lips nervously and swore she could still taste his kiss.

She couldn't answer him or even look at him, she realized as a wave of disappointment washed through her. She couldn't explain herself without risking failing this, if it was a test. With a shake of her head, she rose and walked slowly back toward the house. If she was going to learn how to change her life, then she was going to have to start playing by the rules. If only she knew how.

# CHAPTER TEN

This was getting more difficult, he was starting to care. Mac sighed to himself as he watched Meg move slowly toward the house, her shoulders slumped in weary defeat. He had no idea why she'd ended their kiss, but whatever her reason, it clearly pained her. That pain in her eyes stabbed his chest in an unfamiliar way. He hated seeing her hurt. Even her anger was preferable to the misery radiating from her now.

Mac scowled, his hands clenching in fists. He couldn't help her, he wasn't even sure he could train her anymore. Not like this. He couldn't help noticing the rapid flux of her moods. Each one affected her ability to work magic in different ways. And she *could* work magic, she had more natural power and ability than any dozen apprentices he'd had in the past decade. But her erratic emotions hindered her use of that magic. At the rare times when she was calm, Meg was astonishingly gifted. However, she had trouble grounding and that energy had to go *somewhere*. In Meg, it turned inward, and her mood swung widely from calm to out-of-control.

Mac rubbed his face and smiled ruefully. Unfortunately for his peace of mind, calm was a rare state with Meg. He'd never encountered anyone with her power who wasn't totally controlled. But Meg wasn't. She wanted him, and she wasn't afraid to show it, which was disconcerting, but not nearly as much as her reaction a moment ago. He sighed heavily. With Meg, there was no telling what went through her head. She was an emotional time bomb.

Mac's eyes followed the sway of her ass, and his blood heated. Regardless of her reaction to their kiss, he was well aware of the genesis of her recent mood. He could feel the tension that danced between them like a live circuit. Hell, he should be glad they were alone out here, because only a complete moron wouldn't have noticed the sexual tension around here.

His jaw clenched and he drew deep breaths that did nothing to combat his painful arousal. He wanted Meg so bad he could taste it, and he knew she wanted him, too. He could feel it in her feverish gaze whenever she looked at him. Problem was, they couldn't do anything about this attraction. They couldn't have an affair and do magic at the same time. Their concentration would be broken and… and who the hell was he trying to fool? His concentration, at the very least, was already gone.

Mac groaned at his own stupidity, as realization dawned. The solution to their problem – and Meg's training – was so simple! Why hadn't he thought of it before? When they'd kissed, and shared lifesource, they'd broken the rule he'd been struggling to salvage. He'd never stepped beyond the rules before, and yet, he couldn't manage to feel guilty for his transgression. And why?

Mac sighed heavily. He didn't feel guilty

because, frankly, Meg wasn't like any apprentice he'd ever had, and it had nothing to do with her being a woman. Meg wasn't *meant* to be anyone's apprentice. She was an elemental force in need of simple guidance and balance, not training. None of the ancient rules of apprenticeship applied to Meg. And as long as he was prepared to accept responsibility for his actions, her heritage wasn't an obstacle, either. His breath caught as he realized what it all meant. Meg had been right all along, it was time to throw out the rulebook.

*****

Meg could feel the heat of Mac's gaze burning into her as she strode up the path, her feet crunching on the frozen ground. She tried to tell herself she didn't care what he was thinking, but she knew that was a lie. She was desperate to know she hadn't made a fool of herself again.

She sucked in a breath, but forced herself to not react, as she heard the tromp of Mac's booted feet behind her. He was too quiet and had been since he'd kissed her. But she refused to dwell on it. She was tired and cold, and so not in the mood for any long lectures about rules. She wished Mac would do something to ease the ache in her body – or at least *hold* her – but she wasn't going to beg for what she already knew she couldn't have. Not if she was going to make any progress.

Meg entered the house, and sighed as the

warmth embraced her, chasing away some of her melancholy.  Now, if only she could get away from a certain sex-god charmer for a while…

"We need to talk."

Meg winced.  *Definitely* not what she needed or wanted to hear.

"Isn't that supposed to be *my* line, Mac?"

He looked startled, before a grimness that almost scared her settled over his face.

"This isn't the time to joke, *leannan*," he said somberly as he guided her toward the long, suede sofa near the fireplace and urged her to sit.  The tone of his voice leached away any warmth the roaring fire might have restored, and Meg shivered, chilled to the core by fear.

"All right.  So talk."  She kept her eyes fixed on the fire.  She already knew what was coming, and knowing he felt the need to remind her of the rules, yet again, made her miserable.  She didn't need another lecture on how they weren't supposed to touch, or another reminder that this electric awareness between them was supposed to be wrong.

Damn it, it didn't *feel* wrong!  Ever since she'd first turned to find Mac standing beside her in the coffee shop, she'd felt this insane attraction – something almost unheard of in Meg's life.  She didn't want any more lectures. She wanted to drag Mac off to bed– hell, this sofa would do – and do all those forbidden things that gave her hot, tingly feelings and made her want to scream in frustration at the same time.

She suddenly realized Mac wasn't talking. He was sitting there studying her, his face impassive but his eyes full of a heat that turned Meg's insides into warm Jell-O. He'd wanted to talk. So what was he waiting for, a confession?

Finally, when the stretching silence became oppressive, and that hot, direct gaze began unraveling the calm she was fighting so hard for, Meg sighed heavily and gave in. He wanted an apology? Fine, he could have it.

"Okay. I screwed up out there and almost crossed the line again. Mac, I can't keep—"

"I have an idea," he broke in abruptly in that husky brogue that tripped her pulse.

She couldn't keep thinking of him, *reacting* to him, this way. She had to distract herself before she did something stupid again. She sighed inwardly. Nothing provided better distraction than reciting all those rules she had trouble remembering. In her head, she began listing them off, even as she blandly enquired, "Really? How are we going to solve this problem?"

"First, we're going to make love."

She was up to Rule Nine now. Something about always incanting... Damn, what was it? Distractedly, she nodded her response. "Okay."

"Then we're going to channel your power in a different manner, for your training," he continued, his words a murmur in her ears that didn't really register. "Since your passions are the outlet for your grounding, you need focus, and since the only time you seem to focus is in intimate moments, we can start by turning the initial lessons into sex games."

She nodded vaguely, her attention focused on the elusive Rule Nine. Why couldn't she ever seem to remember this one? If only Mac would quit going on about sex, she might... Meg froze as his words finally pierced the distracted haze, and all the rules flew from her mind as her gaze snapped to his face. "We're *what*?"

*****

Mac's lips twitched as amusement shot through him. He'd known the moment she'd agreed without question that Meg wasn't paying attention. Not entirely.

"I said, we're going to make love."

She blinked and shook her head. "Did I miss something?"

That was an odd response. Mac frowned. "Like what?"

"Like the part where you decided to play this really *un*funny practical joke."

Irritation had been slowly eroding away his amusement at her obtuseness for the past couple of minutes. That last comment snapped his restraint completely. With a muttered oath, he grasped her arms and pulled her against him as he muttered, "I'm not joking. Not even close, *leannan*."

"Really?" She looked utterly unconvinced. "And what happened to the rulebook? Rule Three, remember?"

"Rules change."

"Not that one."  She met his gaze steadily, and he saw strength, and conviction, in her that he'd never seen before.  "Forget it, Mac. I'm not falling for your tricks or your tests."

"Damn it, Meg!"  He surged from the sofa, dragging her with him, and yanked her close until they were pressed so tightly together not even a breath would fit between them. Grasping her hand, he brought it against his fly, his jaw tightening against a groan as her soft hand instinctively cupped him.  Forcing the words past a throat tight with want, he rasped, "Does that feel like a joke to you?"

He met her gaze, and nearly drowned in the soft, vulnerable depths of honey-brown as they grew wide, her pupils dilating with arousal.  She licked her lips, and blood surged in his groin.  Spirits of Shadow, she was killing him with that look!

"No," she finally admitted in a breathless whisper.  "But I don't understand…"

He released her hand, lifting his own to cup her neck, his thumb feathering over her cheek as he softly explained, "Though, for reasons I can't tell you yet, this is going to have to continue to appear as an apprenticeship to the rest of the *Strata*, Meg, I can't tutor you."

She backed away a step, and the betrayal in her eyes stung worse than it should have. "Because you want to have sex with me."

"No!  I mean, yes, but… oh, *ifrinn*."  He stopped, drew a ragged breath.  "Look, it's complicated."

A wry smile tugged at her lips.  "I don't see

how. You either want me or you don't."

"Oh, I want you, *leannan*," he whispered against her ear, before licking the hollow just beneath it lightly. She moaned and arched her head slightly, and Mac's pulse sped. "And I intend to have you."

She froze. "Mac, the lessons…"

"Will continue." He offered her a reassuring smile, before dipping his head to taste the skin where her collarbones met. "Think of it as foreplay."

She jumped as his hand skimmed up the inside of her jeans-clad thighs, and Mac felt triumph swell, along with his already painful hard-on. He'd bet anything she was slick beneath those jeans. He rubbed his hand over the seam of her pants for a moment, until she gasped and stiffened, and then moved his hand higher, slowly sliding down the tab of her jeans.

"Mac?" Her breathless query stopped him.

"Aye?"

"Is this a lesson?"

She looked uncertain, and vulnerable, and Mac realized his error immediately. Meg wasn't sure what to make of the rules being upended on her. For all the chaos she'd grown up in, Meg was very conscious of the rules, once they settled in. She might push an issue to see how far she could bend things, but at heart, Meg wasn't any more of a rule breaker than he was. Mac smiled, liking that similarity.

"Relax," he murmured as he stroked a finger lightly down her cheek and neck. Feral pleasure wound through him as she shivered and moaned in response. "We don't have to make a lesson of this first time. I just need to see you," his voice dropped to a rumble, his words hissing out as he slipped his hands beneath her sweater and resisted the urge to groan with pleasure. "To feel you."

Her breathing quickened, and he watched her eyes dilate further. Then, she licked her lips nervously.

"I…" She swallowed visibly as she met his gaze. "I think I *need* it to be, Mac."

He saw the mingling of want and fear in her eyes and understood. She didn't like feeling vulnerable, and not having a deal between them would leave her vulnerable. Mac smiled softly and bent his head to breathe in the sweet, yet spicy, scent of her. He skimmed his lips over the pulse point where her shoulder and neck joined, and felt her little jump, even as she gasped. "Why?"

She dragged in an uneven breath, and he could feel the thunder of her pulse against his lips as he lingered, tasting her skin.

"Because otherwise, I'm going to scream," she admitted in a husky murmur, her words blunt enough Mac knew she was nervous. He chuckled as he trailed his hand lower, over the soft wool of her sweater, until he could delve his hands beneath the hem again, to curve against her waist.

"Oh, I assure you, *leannan*," he growled thickly as his body responded to the brush of bare flesh. He yanked her flush against him, knowing she could feel the thrust of his confined erection against her belly. "By the time we're through, you'll scream– lesson or not."

With that promise, he took possession of her delectable mouth, already aware he was offering himself as her prisoner.

*****

He'd promised to make her scream. Meg nearly fainted with need at the mere thought of how he might plan to do that. As Mac's tongue teased her lips lightly, she opened hungrily to his probing. The instant she did, everything changed. Gone was the playful skim of his fingers and the butterfly-light kisses. Mac's mouth claimed hers, his tongue delving and torturing her until she squirmed and moaned with need. But his hands weren't moving. Instead, his grip on her waist tightened, holding her pressed against him as he devoured her mouth, driving her crazy. She moaned again, her hand smoothing over his chest and down.

She yanked away after a moment to mutter, "Dammit, Mac. *Touch* me."

His bronze eyes met hers, bright with hunger and amusement.

"How do you want me to touch you, Meg?" His murmur feathered over her throat as he skimmed soft kisses there.

"I don't care. Just touch." She couldn't believe this! She was burning up with lust, and he wanted to *talk*?

"You wanted a lesson," he reminded her in a husky growl against her ear as he suddenly turned her, the fire's light casting her shadow against the wall before her. "Don't *tell* me where you want me to touch you, or how. *Show* me."

Her eyes widened in surprise. He wasn't serious! She turned her head toward him. He wasn't telling her to... "You want me to touch myself? Here? In *front* of you?"

"No." Amusement threaded his voice. "I want you to focus and use our shadows to show me what you want."

A little thrill shot through her. What he was suggesting was dangerous for both of them. He was giving her control of his shadow, and instinctively, she knew that meant he had to give up control of his power as well. She wasn't sure how she knew, it was just one of those things she knew without a doubt. She was going to have to use her power to bring all of her fantasies to life, and he would be able to do nothing but watch. It was frightening and exhilarating. A tingle coursed her veins, and her nipples tightened with anticipation. She could do this. She knew she could.

Her gaze focused on the shadows before her, and something inside of her stretched out, filling the flat, lifeless shadows with animation. She watched in fascination as her shadow-self slowly stepped away from the wall becoming almost solid. At the same time, Mac's shadow stepped off the wall as well.

*Meg turned to Mac and smiled as she peeled away her sweater, revealing bare, shadowed curves. She tossed her head back, midnight hair spilling down as Mac cupped her breasts and lowered his head to taste their tips. Her hands pulled at his shirt, steadily divesting him of it.*

Meg's palms tingled as if her fingers lay against Mac's flesh and lightning shot from her breasts to her core with the feel of Mac's touch, though there was almost a foot of space between them now. Watching their shadows, she knew she was feeling everything through her shadow, and that Mac felt it as well. A wry smile tugged at her lips. It was like interactive porn, without the cheesy music. Just the sounds of their breathing, and the pounding of two hearts.

*Meg backed away suddenly, and her hands dropped to Mac's waist as she unfastened his jeans and pushed them away to gain access. She slid her mouth over his chest and down.*

Mac, standing beside her, straightened suddenly as he sucked in a sharp breath. Meg smiled wickedly, knowing he could feel everything, and was surprised when her shadow counterpart did the same.

*Meg dropped to her knees, her hands cupping Mac's impressively hard shaft as she leaned in and ran her tongue over it.*

Meg heard a strangled sound halfway between a groan and an oath leave the man beside her, but couldn't tear her eyes away from the sight of their shadows as heat thrummed through her. She could *feel* him, taste the salt of his flesh in her mouth.

"Enough." His voice sounded rough as he turned and yanked Meg to him, his eyes full of dangerous heat as he ground out, "What are you

Meg's gaze flickered, and Mac felt the shift of shadows that danced around them. Warm shade enfolded him, before the cooler air of the cabin suddenly brushed against his skin, and he realized Meg was using the skill he'd been trying to teach her outside to divest him of his shirt.

"Nice," she murmured, her voice a honeyed purr that nearly reduced his control to non-existent. Her hands left the sofa to cover his on her breasts and then slide slowly up his now-bare arms and over his chest. She leaned into his stroking hands as her own mimicked his motions against his chest. Her warm breath feathered against his skin, and she touched her lips to his ear as she murmured, "Forget about the screaming. Just take me to bed."

Like hell, he would. His fantasies revolved around watching this woman come apart in the passion he created. And if there was one thing Alasdair MacCorran always kept, it was his promises. Before the night was over, the entire *Strata* would hear Meg's cry of pleasure. It was a promise he was looking forward to keeping.

## CHAPTER ELEVEN

Meg sighed and stretched, reveling in her nakedness and the sense of satiation that snuggled around her like a warm blanket. She'd never felt better in her life, it didn't even bother her they'd made love on the thick, bearskin rug in front of the fire, instead of a proper bed. She felt deliciously wicked.

Warm skin shifted against hers from behind, and a large hand skimmed over her belly and breasts. Meg turned her head to offer Mac a smile as she snuggled back against him. "That was amazing."

His bronze eyes glinted in the firelight as they met hers from beneath the wild locks of dark hair she'd mussed with her hands, in the throes of the most intense sexual experience of her life. He looked like a pirate, with shadows flickering over his face, and fire dancing in his eyes. Her heart leapt, and her body clenched with renewed need as his lips tilted in a rakish smile.

"It's you who's amazing, *leannan*," he whispered as he trailed his lips slowly down her throat, his hand dipping lower.

"Mac." She stopped his hand, and his gaze came back to her face, his expression suddenly concerned. "Why can I only use magic when we have sex?"

He sighed as he shifted and rose up on his elbow, his gaze on the fire. "I have a theory."

Those words struck Meg in the chest, and

convinced the man who could slay his brother would somehow find her, as well. Foolish, really, but she'd been an easily – frightened child. "Yeah, I've heard the story."

"The story says Cain was marked by his deity for his crime, so all humanity would know what he had done. I found references to similar markings in other texts and histories of your world."

She nodded. "*The Scarlet Letter* comes to mind. And heretics during the Inquisition were often marked with a symbol – usually a cross – burned into their faces or bodies."

"Aye."

"So what's that got to do with our situation?"

He sighed heavily. "In the *Strata*, the laws of the *Lux Magica* – that is, the Light Magics – are determined and enforced by a council known as the *Illuminata*. Those who knowingly break the laws held as proper conduct for *Magi* can be given the Mark, that is, an indelible bloodstain on the left half of their faces. Marked ones are shunned and not permitted to use the *Strata*. Often, they become agents of a darker force."

Meg's breath caught. "Why would they do that to you?"

"Because you are a very special woman, Meg, and I knew better than to touch you."

"And how do you know who I am?"

He sighed. "After you left the coffeehouse that day, all the power went out, and your boss claimed it was your fault."

Meg winced. Ever since the day she'd blown up the coffee machine after he'd got in her face for no reason, Phil the Pill had blamed her for every mishap. She couldn't defend herself against the accusations, either. She wasn't sure she wasn't to blame, herself.

"How's that prove anything?"

He chuckled. "It sparked my interest, *leannan*. Before that, you'd only proved yourself uncontrolled and thus unfit for training. But that incident told me you had untapped power that needed training and quickly." He smiled, shaking his head ruefully. "I just didn't realize at the time that it wasn't malleable power. I thought I could train you."

"When did you change your mind?"

"On the ride up."

She blinked, startled. He'd known something about her past *that* long ago? "That's one hell of a secret to keep, Mac."

"I know, but I didn't have a choice. You wouldn't have believed me if I'd told you."

She narrowed her eyes. "I'm not sure I do now, either. How did you decide I was different?"

His smile softened as he raised his hands to lightly frame her face. "You have the eyes of an *Illuminata*."

She jerked away from his touch as uneasiness stabbed through her. Hadn't he just said the *Illuminata* were lawmakers and enforcers in his world? "*Excuse* me? You're saying I'm an *Illumi* whatever, but I don't even know what that is."

his hands sliding to her waist. "We're not done."

"Damn straight," she muttered breathlessly as her hands dipped between their bodies to work at the fastening of his jeans.

Gods of Shadow, she was going to drive him crazy! He groaned and reached to still her hands. "You asked about magic."

She stilled, and he watched wariness cross her face. "What about it?"

"You wanted to know why it only works when we make love." He met her eyes levelly and saw the distracted light there. She wasn't going to like this. "It only works then because that's the only time you're focused enough."

Suddenly, his arms were empty, and Meg was pacing away from him. "I'm focused."

"No, you're not. Your energies are scattered by your confusion and your masks. The only time they come together is when you let yourself go and tune your attention to something else." He sighed and offered her a rueful, apologetic smile. "That shadow display earlier was proof enough. You were so focused on my reactions and your own pleasure, you almost convinced *me* those images and sensations were real."

She paced restlessly for several moments, and he watched her silently, aware of her struggle and her need for space, though his body cried out to have her close again. She didn't want to believe he was right, but she did. Finally, she sighed in disgust and whipped about to face him.

"All right.  So, how do I learn to focus with*out* sex?"

He grinned.  That she'd rallied so quickly didn't surprise him.  He'd expected it.

"I have an idea.  But, it'll keep for tonight." He met her gaze, and let her read the heat in his, the need he felt for her.  "Come here."

*****

Finnagas grinned smugly as the woman beside him in the coach stared at the mansion, her expression frozen.

"Admit it, cousin.  You feel the energy, and you know what it means as well as I do."

Her lavender eyes turned to him, stormy with emotions she was unable to control.  Poor little Valentina.  She'd always had such appalling lack of control, for a sorceress.

"It doesn't mean *anything*, Finn!  He's got a new apprentice, everyone knows that.  She's been around almost a year.  Besides, Alasdair wouldn't break the rules, and he's in love with *me*."

Finnagas laughed.  She was so delusional. "No apprentice makes a power spike like that, alone!"

She continued to glare at him.  "You're wrong.  I'll prove it."

As she reached for the door handle, Finnagas' hand shot out, stopping her.  "Let's make a wager, my dear cousin.  You go to him tomorrow.  If Alasdair MacCorran takes you back with open arms, I'll give you my

physical gestures and verbal words, women must be able to visualize their objective in their minds. It eventually becomes second nature, but the process takes practice."

Meg glanced down at their joined hands, and her heart lodged in her throat. It looked so right, his larger hand engulfing hers. She felt complete. She swallowed hard, forcing the thought aside, and managed, "How's a handful of pebbles going to help do that?"

He flashed her the same roguish grin he'd given her last night, nearly stopping her heart, even as he lifted her captive hand to his lips. "Most beginners find tactile visualization easiest. Connecting with something through touch allows them to see it easier in their minds."

A mischievous smile curved on her lips. Tactile contact, huh? "You sure we need to use rocks, Mac? I can think of better things…"

He shot her a stern glance, though his eyes sparkled with contained laughter. He bent close, his mouth grazing her neck before he whispered against her ear, "Behave. I know what I'm doing."

Those words were pure sin in her ear. Meg shivered in delight, knowing she could use whatever she learned here to drive him crazy later. Biting back her grin, she sighed in mock resignation.

"Oh, all right." She turned her head to smile at him. "Tell me what you want me to do."

"I've been waiting to hear you say that," he

murmured suggestively, sending a spike of need through Meg, and then chuckled as she shifted. "Close your eyes, *leannan*."

Meg did as instructed. Her heart raced at the knowledge of how vulnerable she left herself. The memory of the last time she'd been blindfolded in front of Mac rushed through her, stirring momentary panic. But Mac was here, and she trusted him now. She felt safe, her awareness heightened by his proximity and her lack of sight. She could feel the heat pouring from Mac, and his presence cocooned her in a safety net that reached clear to her soul. Mac wouldn't let her come to harm. In the next instant, she jerked up slightly as she felt a smooth darkness slide over her face, and a tingle of apprehension ran through her.

"Relax." Mac's warm, brogue-laden voice against her ear made Meg shiver with rippling awareness.

"Easy for you to say," she muttered without rancor.

His deep chuckle stirred her blood, and her nipples tightened with a surge of need, surprising Meg. How did he affect her so easily?

"Not as easy as you think, *m'calman*."

Meg's pulse tripped. He was saying… what, exactly? That she affected him, too? That he was as turned on by the idea of her being blindfolded as she was? She felt Mac's free hand suddenly curve around her waist and jumped.

"What're you doing?"

four boulders roughly the size of bowling balls. Mac's husky encouragements floated through her mind as she did.

"That's it." He gave her a gentle squeeze. "Now, I want you to take those stones and visualize them at the bottom of the pond. See them resting sedately at the bottom of the icy water." His voice purred over her, and she was sinking, along with the rocks. Only, her water was warm and enveloping, and felt like heaven.

Her breathing grew shallow with each word that washed over her, and lassitude and awareness settled over her simultaneously, stirring a strangely calm, but erotic, sensation within her. She was enveloped in warm, peaceful darkness, safe from the world's prying eyes, and she felt free.

"That's it. Now, scoop the rocks into your hands and lift them toward the surface."

Meg shot toward the surface as the need to finish the exercise and immerse herself in the peaceful feeling again roared through her.

"Damn it! Ease up, Meg! You'll—"

A misting spray of water followed the sound of splintering ice, and Meg felt icy water sprinkle against her face.

"Hold that." Mac's command hissed near her ear, even as the blindfold disappeared and she felt him withdraw angrily. "Now, open your eyes and see what your impatience has done."

Reluctantly, Meg opened her eyes, and gasped as disbelief poured through her. *She* had done this? Four boulders – roughly the size of bowling balls – hung, spinning, in midair. There was no way…

"No!" Mac's warning came a split second too late as the balls of rock dropped hard, hitting the surface of the pond with enough force to send a wave of icy water jetting up and over Meg, drenching her before she could get out of its path.

Meg screeched and backpedaled futilely as the wave of icy water poured over her. She was soaked to the skin, her clothes clinging wetly to her in the freezing cold. She shivered, and then shuddered, as the icy wind bit into her, and her teeth began to chatter. She clutched her arms around her body, but couldn't find any warmth.

"Meg!" Mac was suddenly at her side, his expression full of concern. "Are you all right?"

"I… I'm c-cold," she managed through chattering teeth.

Mac's arms enveloped her, and she felt the heat of his body seep through her chill as his hands ran over her body in an attempt to dry her with his power.

"This isn't something I usually do," he whispered against her ear, and she saw his flickering attempt at humor.

She tried to stop shivering, to assure him she was all right. But the cold sank to her bones, and she couldn't banish it. Her legs trembled and nearly gave out.

"You have to stay standing, *leannan*," he ordered briskly, even as he dropped to his knees on the snowy ground at her feet. "If you collapse, you'll drain yourself automatically, in

## CHAPTER THIRTEEN

"Valentina!"

Meg heard the shock – and was that guilt? In Mac's voice as he released her and surged to his feet in one sift move.    Painful disbelief plunged into her, twisting like a knife as she realized Mac knew this woman and, by the feral, possessive gleam in the woman's lavender eyes, he knew her in the biblical sense.  So, who was she and, more importantly, what was she to Mac?  The disturbing possibility that she had spent last night in the arms of a married man made Meg nauseous.  God.  She'd thought Mac was different…

"Mac?"   She backed away from him, the query slipping from her lips in a hoarse whisper.   She wanted him to deny it, she realized.   She wanted him to introduce this woman as a relative or platonic friend, *anything* but wife or girlfriend.

Mac's bronze eyes met hers, and she read the anger and fear there, and knew.  He wasn't going to deny it.

Oh, God.  Ohgodohgodohgod…

"Meg, go up to the house and change into some warm, dry clothes," he instructed in a quiet voice that sent anger tripping through Meg.  She was being dismissed like an errant child!

"So you can be alone with Ms. Sex Kitten, there?"  She snapped, letting her glare travel from the sensually made-up Valentina to Mac, where it froze. "You must think I'm *really* dumb."

His jaw clenched, and she could see the muscles in his face working overtime before his gaze clashed with hers, practically screaming at her to not question him. Oh, he'd like that, would he? Not feeling particularly charitable, Meg sent him back a look that told him to not hold his breath. She wasn't about to make things easy on him.

"I'm staying right here," she reiterated, only barely keeping her teeth from chattering in the process.

"You're freezing," he argued calmly, totally ignoring Valentina's presence.

"How appropriate. You're ice."

"Meg," he ground out from between clenched teeth, his calm composure slipping a little. "I'm not going to argue with you. You're my apprentice, you do exactly as I say. Now, go back to the house and change."

Those words slapped Meg hard, nearly sending her stumbling back into the pond as the truth weakened her locked knees. His *apprentice*? Oh, God. That meant he'd used her. He was saying she was nothing but a toy, to him.

Meg's eyes narrowed as her spine stiffened. Well, to hell with him. He could tell himself all the stories he wanted to, she knew he'd wanted her and badly. She fully intended to remind him, too, just as soon as they were alone again. No matter *who* Valentina was, Mac owed Meg more than a brush-off. He owed her the truth.

to push his luck with a *Faladibhe*– a vampiric – when in a rage. But he couldn't bite back the scornful laugh that flew from his lips, or a muttered, "You don't hold a candle to Meg."

Valentina's face blanched, and her entire bearing took on a sinister cast. A spike of apprehension lanced through Mac. Her *Faladibhe* blood was definitely showing now. He'd best be watching his neck.

"That mewling strumpet of an apprentice, you mean? You're *screwing* her?"

Thoughts for safety flew from his mind as rage bit sharply into Mac's heart. He clenched his fists, containing it. He wasn't about to show Valentina anything except cold, hard indifference. He would never let her see she'd pricked him, or his protective instincts.

"You always were crude gutter trash," he said coldly. "And what happens between myself and Meg is no concern of yours."

Her dark laugh sent ice shooting along Mac's spine. She sounded like a *Saguis Domini*!

"That's what *you* think, Alasdair," she cooed again, the sound ominous rather than sweet. "But I can take my misused honor to the *Illuminata*. I'll tell them you promised your loyalty to me, and then turned to the arms of a common gutterbrand, and made her your apprentice as payment for her services." She slunk a step closer, her eyes hot with malice. "I can destroy you. I can have you Marked, and that mewling strumpet executed."

Those final words drove a spike of terror, and rage, through Mac, snapping his control.

His fists clenched and he ground out, "If you say so much as a *word* against Meg—"

She laughed scornfully, her eyes telling him he'd given himself away, before she sashayed back toward the road, where a dark carriage, pulled by three black alacorns, awaited her. Over her shoulder, she tossed her parting shot.

"Don't look now, darling, but your Achilles' heel is showing. You have until *Luna Ascesa* to change your mind, or nothing you do will protect your precious little Meg."

*****

Mac mulled over Valentina's threat the whole way back to the house. He wasn't worried about his own reputation – compared to the Crawfords, his family position and his personal reputation were pristine. But Meg was unknown in the *Strata*. They would blame her for the affair, and claim she used a Siren's wiles to lead one of their respected *Draoi* astray. Mac's gut churned at the thought of how she could suffer. He'd chosen Meg for his apprentice because of a bet. It had been pure whim. He'd toyed with her life, and now she was facing possible ridicule from the very people he'd promised her would accept her with open arms.

Guilt stirred in Mac. He'd done this, and now he had to *un*do it, for Meg's sake. The *Illuminata* must never have grounds to suspect Valentina's accusation to be true. Mac dragged in a deep breath and felt the cold air slice his

breast in a possessive move, palming her stiff nipple and dragging a needy moan from her. She flexed against him, her kiss suddenly ravenous.

Mac broke their kiss with a growl as he dragged her head back further and buried his mouth against the column of her neck, nipping and laving the pulse there until Meg loosed a small cry, her nails digging into his shoulders as she panted, "Mac…please…"

His hands released her, and he yanked the robe from her body as her eager hands tore at the fastenings of his shirt and jeans. He opened his eyes to the hunger in her honey-brown gaze, and the last thread of his control snapped.

Hot blood pounding in his veins, Mac was aware of nothing except his need for Meg. He scooped her into his arms and pressed her against the door as he thrust her flimsy, barely-there negligee up and bent his head to suck her turgid nipple into his mouth. He bit down lightly, and felt her arch toward him, even as his fingers delved into her hot, creamy center. Her hips bucked in response, and she uttered a tiny sound halfway between a moan and a cry.

Need and want slammed through Mac simultaneously as her capable hands wrapped around his cock, stroking in a way that nearly drove him insane. He drove his fingers to the hilt in her body, dragging a desperate cry from her as she arched into his touch, writhing against the door. Her head tipped back and her breasts thrust out, their tips rosy and glistening from his attentions, even as her hands pumped his engorged flesh in a rhythm that was pure heaven. He groaned, his eyes nearly rolling back. But he couldn't stop watching her.

Mac's heart thundered. The sight of Meg's ecstasy held him so spellbound he couldn't turn away, or close his eyes to absorb the sensation of her touch. He watched her face instead, the awe and pleasure that grew there as his fingers stroked in and out and his thumb tortured her sensitive clit.

As she suddenly stilled, and he felt a tremble work through her body, her flesh tightening around his fingers, he knew he couldn't hold back any longer. He had to be in her. Withdrawing his fingers, he let her guide him home, to burrow in her warm, welcoming flesh, and his groan of pleasure matched hers.

*****

Meg arched against Mac, her legs wrapping tightly around his waist, at the exquisite sensation of fullness. Digging her nails into his shoulders, she offered her breasts, and gasped with the rush of sensation as his mouth closed over one, and electricity shot from her nipple to her womb.

"Mac." She flexed her hips and felt him shudder, before he thrust again, rocketing her toward the stratosphere, tightening the thread of delicious need until it snapped, and she fell into an orgasm that left her trembling and weak with aftershocks.

## CHAPTER FOURTEEN

Meg tossed the small, shadowy ball between her hands and offered Mac an impish grin. This was getting easier every day!

"I did it!" She exalted, and watched soft humor bloom in his eyes as a smile touched his lips. "I actually did it!"

Mac propped a hip against the edge of the piano, his gaze steady on her. "I knew you could. You've been learning quickly. This was the final lesson, in bending magic to create what you need."

She laughed as she tossed the ball toward him and reordered the fall of her robe as she drew her legs up onto the window seat. "And what do I need with a ball?"

"Nothing," he replied easily as he caught the shadowy sphere with one hand. "Yet you managed to create one."

Meg's gaze fastened on his hands, his long, tapered fingers moving slowly over the grapefruit sized ball with the same sensuality he'd applied to her breast earlier. She swallowed hard as a tingle of want ran through her, tightening her nipples and twisting her womb with drenching need. They'd spent more time in bed than out of it, for the past two weeks. He'd taught her to manipulate shadows, using the most amazing sex play she'd ever experienced. When she recalled his lessons in balancing light and shadow, her body quaked with raw hunger. And her blood still sang from his lesson in bending magic.

"Meg?"

The husky quality of his voice drew her gaze to his face, and she saw the flare of heat in his eyes. She couldn't speak, held under that mesmerizing gaze. Wordlessly, she held out her arms, inviting him. She sighed with pleasure as he scooped her from the window seat and carried her up the stairs, his expression so resolute, she couldn't resist a tiny, nervous giggle.

"Mac, we don't have to use a bed…"

His scorching gaze silenced her, before he rasped, "I have no intention of using the bed. At least, not at first."

Meg's heart stalled, and she sucked in a shallow breath as her nipples tightened nearly to the point of pain, needing his touch. She wanted to ask what he *did* intend, but couldn't work the words past her throat.

*****

Three hours later, Meg had her answer. Mac had intended, and succeeded marvelously, to make her boneless with satiation. After the most stimulating bath of her life, in water scented like heaven and sin combined, he'd dried her carefully, leaving not a single inch of her uncovered by the towel's soft stroke. Then he'd finally carried her to the bed, where he'd made love to her with an intensity she'd never experienced. Meg shuddered pleasantly, her nipples tightening in renewed excitement at the memory. Mac had shown her what it felt like to be cherished. Eyes closed, she swallowed hard as she faced the truth. She *didn't* want just his body. She wanted it all. She wanted him to feel what she did. She wanted him to love her.

Opening her eyes, she watched Mac toy with her fingers, each stroking motion tightening her throat. Mac never noticed, he was totally absorbed in his task of petting and manipulating her fingers. Meg frowned. He'd been acting strange ever since that day out at the pond. What had that woman said to him? What had those moments after he'd banished her to the house done to him? Mac wasn't usually evasive or moody, that she'd ever noticed, but he was steadily becoming both with every day that passed.

With an exasperated sigh, she decided she'd had enough of his maudlin mood. As good as he made her feel, she wasn't about to sit still for deception.

"All right. Since we haven't covered telepathy, that I recall, you're going to have to *tell* me what's bothering you." She withdrew her hand from his grasp and shifted up on her elbow, forcing him to look up to meet her gaze.

He shrugged. "Nothing you need to worry about."

Her eyes narrowed, and she leveled the first of her suspicions at him. "Are you married?"

Mac's eyes widened in shock, before insulted anger pulsed through the bronze. "Of course not."

"Engaged?" That would be par for the course. Her first boyfriend had been a weasel who thought that, because he wasn't married *yet*, he wasn't in a committed relationship.

Mac's anger turned to hurt, then derision. "Don't be absurd."

Meg's anger – fed by frustration – pricked her hard. "Well, then. Who was that woman you spoke to out at the pond a couple of weeks ago?"

He grimaced and shrugged. "No one important."

"Then why are you moping?"

"I am not."

"Really? You mean these past two weeks are normal, and what came before that was the aberration?" She couldn't help the sarcastic bite of her words. She was getting damned sick of his evasions.

Mac was silent, studying her, before he sighed heavily. "*Luna Ascesa* is in three days."

She vaguely remembered him mentioning that, the day they'd met, and again the day after the pond incident. But she couldn't recall him explaining what it *meant*, or why it worried him so much.

"What is that?"

His hand stretched out, and his fingers trailed over her bare shoulder and down the outside of her arm, sending a shiver of pleasure through Meg.

"*Luna Ascesa*," he murmured thoughtfully, his gaze focused on his finger's trek, "is the biggest gala and trade conference of the *Strata*.

Every Master and Mistress of magical arts is required to attend."

Meg laid her hand over his, halting him. She met his gaze steadily as, in a murmur, she asked, "And why does this worry you so much?"

He refused to meet her gaze, his expression more troubled than before. "It's not just a party, Meg. It's a time for the trade of information between disciplines."

"I'm still not seeing the problem."

He shifted, and his eyes closed, as if he fought the words that slipped from his lips. "Each Master and Mistress chooses his or her most promising apprentice to perform in a special competition. It's a display of innovation, and proof that the knowledge and traditions are being passed on."

Meg froze, her heart stalling mid-beat as an icy chill spread through her body. "*Every* apprentice?"

His nod was stiff, and his expression grim as he continued to avoid her gaze. "Aye."

Panic tripped through Meg. She was Mac's *only* apprentice that she knew of. Surely, he didn't intend to go through with this!

"We're not going, right?"

His bronze eyes met hers at last, and Meg felt panic scream through her as she saw the answer burning there, even before he said, "I'm required to attend, Meg."

The fist of panic tightened. "Okay. Then I'll just stay here and—"

"You have to go with me, *leannan*," he

murmured, his voice soft with apology. "You're the only apprentice I have."

Her eyes closed, Meg fought the strangling grasp of entrapment. She couldn't do this, Meg avoided the spotlight her parents craved, deliberately. Mac wouldn't ask her to step into it, not if he cared about her at all. "What does that mean?"

His fingers skimmed her cheek, and she opened her eyes to see the apology and pain in his. "You have to perform, *m'calman*."

The panic froze in her chest, and snapped as rage pushed through. Mac was supposed to *care*, dammit! Fury flashed in her as she yanked away from him and leapt from the bed. "I'm *not* a trained monkey, Mac!"

He sat up as well, and a frown flashed across his face. "I never said you were."

"Yeah, right."

"Meg, what is this? I know you're not pleased, but—"

"You don't know anything!" She railed at him, and shook her head sharply. "Of course you don't understand. I'm nothing but a diversion for you."

He stiffened abruptly. "That's not—"

"Do you *hear* yourself, MacCorran?" She snapped as she yanked her robe from the floor and belted it tightly in angry motions. "I have to 'perform'."

Her sneered use of the word made it deliberately crude, and she watched him wince, before anger settled over his features. Good. She was spoiling for a fight.

"I meant *magic*, Meg. As my apprentice, you have to give a display of what you've learned from me."

She barked out a laugh. "It's a little difficult to demonstrate betrayal, Mac."

He froze, and his eyes blazed, but his voice was lethally quiet as he said, "Betrayal? I've never betrayed you, Megara."

"*Don't*," she warned, holding onto her anger with every ounce of self-preservation she possessed. There was no way he was explaining *this* slap away. "Don't even use that name."

"Meg…"

She stalked to the window, hoping the motion would disguise the pained tremble radiating from her heart out. Damn him, he'd known this all along and hadn't bothered to tell her. He'd made love to her, made her love him, and he'd been lying to her all along.

"This wasn't part of our deal," she said stiffly, staring out at the snow-covered mountainside. Her heart felt like it was buried out there, under the snowdrifts.

"Actually, it was," he argued quietly, even as he leaned back against the headboard. "You have to remain with me until the Second of January, remember? That's the last day of *Luna Ascesa*."

"You tricked me!" She accused, whirling on him as she fought back tears.

He sighed heavily. "You never asked why I was so specific about the date, either. If I'd known it was such a problem, I would have told you sooner."

She glared at him. "How convenient. And, of course, that explains why I had to drag it out of you now."

Anger and frustration flashed in his eyes. "Damn it, Meg! By the time I realized how much it might matter, I couldn't fix the problem. I was afraid I'd lose you, if I told you."

Fresh pain stabbed Meg. He was right, he couldn't fix this problem. She closed her eyes, feeling vulnerable and exposed in ways that had nothing to do with her state of near nakedness. She'd been a fool. Even demanding to know the rules ahead of time, she'd proved herself no better than Faust, or her parents, in the end. She'd still fallen for the Devil's trap – even worse, she'd fallen into his bed and let him have her heart. Crossing her arms protectively over the aching void in her chest, she turned back to the window.

"Fine," she finally said, nodding stiffly as emptiness engulfed her. "I'll go. But you'd better train me how to do this shadow stuff without any more sex."

He was already halfway out of bed. "Meg…"

"You were right about one thing," she said quietly. "You can't fix this."

She turned and, avoiding Mac's gaze, strode out his bedroom door. She wouldn't be back, if she could avoid it. She prayed she was that strong.

*****

Mac stared at the closed door as Meg's final words pierced him clear to the soul. The pain surprised him. He'd never felt this kind of clutching panic when a relationship ended before. But the idea of Meg walking out of his life after *Luna Ascesa* tightened his chest with a pain that couldn't be pushed aside. He'd give anything – even his magic and his reputation, to keep her by his side. With a sharply indrawn breath, he realized why. Sometime since he'd first looked into her eyes back at the *Hole In the Wall*, he'd let her slip into his heart. He'd fallen for her.

Mac swore beneath his breath as he faced another truth. Meg was right, he'd betrayed her. He'd let her believe he was giving her a chance to change her life and instead, he'd been training her with the sole purpose of salvaging his own reputation and his family's honor. That his purpose had changed, and he cared about Meg's future and her happiness, was something he'd never had a chance to argue. And now, it looked like he never would.

## CHAPTER FIFTEEN

Today was the day. Meg paced the sitting room in wide circles, deliberately avoiding looking at the thick bearskin rug. She couldn't bear the heartbreaking memories of this place any longer. Had she been headed anywhere except *Luna Ascesa*, she'd be relieved to get away from any reminders of Mac and what he made her feel. Meg quickened her steps. Maybe, if she moved fast enough, she could outrun her jumbled emotions, forget Mac, and—

"You need to calm down."

Meg whirled at the sound of Mac's voice, to find the man in question standing in the sitting room archway. Her gaze slid over his dark silk shirt – a shade of green she supposed qualified as olive – and black leather pants and jacket, and dropped quickly to his motorcycle boots as she fought down a surge of heat. He'd never looked so good, and she'd never felt so desperate before. He wanted her to be calm? She uttered a disbelieving laugh.

"Screw you," she shot back.

His chuckle shot through her tightly strung nerves, and the flare in his eyes told her she'd just made a tactical error. "Was that an offer, *leannan*?"

"No!"

"That was a joke, Meg. Lighten up." There was a definite edge of hurt to his tone. God, she didn't want to think about it.

"I'm not the one who lied," she reminded

him quietly.

She resumed pacing, too wound up to stay motionless. She needed to *move*, or she'd go crazy. She heard Mac's sigh, before she suddenly found her path blocked by six-foot-three of silk-and-leather clad man. She glared up at him, even as her heart tripped. "Move."

"Meg…"

She opened her mouth, intent on telling him off. Her glare clashed with the tender exasperation in his eyes, and the effect was like a kick in the ribs. She couldn't breathe, under the force of his gaze. Her heart hammered, and her brain grew fuzzy. Her anger slid from her grasp steadily, in spite of her stubborn grip on it. She wanted to blame him, to label it some spell he'd placed on her. Only, she knew quite well Mac's magic couldn't influence – couldn't even *touch* – the human heart or soul, just as she knew he'd never use it, even if he could. She summoned up her most forbidding scowl, anyway.

"Don't look at me like that, dammit!"

To his credit, Mac didn't even attempt innocence. Instead, his lips quirked wryly. "Why not?"

Irritation coiled in her until she wanted to scream. She saw the gleam in his eyes and knew he saw her mounting frustration and found it amusing. She refused to be his entertainment, damn him. With a dark glare, she planted her fists on her hips and got in his face instead.

"Because I want to be mad at you, Alasdair MacCorran! I want to be so furious I can hate you. You *lied* to me!"

"Never," he argued quietly, all trace of humor gone from his face.

He wasn't getting away with sincerity either. "You never told me I'd have to *perform* for anyone!"

"True.    But nor did I ever say you *wouldn't*."

Meg clenched her hands together because if she made fists, one of them was going to land squarely in that blandly unconcerned face of Mac's. With a growl of frustration, she stalked away until the window brought her up short.

"A lie of omission is still a lie, Mac." She stared bleakly out the window. "Now what do I do?"

"You put a smile on your face, hold your head up and march into that conference as the bold, confident Meg I know," he said quietly. She heard his booted step on the hard wood and felt his steadying presence envelope her, even before his arms did.    Against her will, her treacherous body sought comfort in his embrace, and she sank against him.

He was wrong. She wasn't bold, and she wasn't confident.    She'd bluffed her way through life, convincing everyone else she was strong and capable, that she'd chosen the life she lived.    But Meg knew the truth, she had no illusions about herself. The real Meg was scared and shy, and weak. The real Meg had been beaten at life so often she no longer believed she was capable.

"I can't do this," she whispered painfully, more to herself than the man behind her.

"You'll do fine," he murmured against her ear, warming Meg in spite of her fears. "In two days, you mastered what I laid out for your performance. You're ready for this, *m'gradh*. As ready as any other apprentice, more ready than you believe."

She sighed and a chill settled over her. It was the cold grip of panic. His assurances weren't having the effect she imagined he was looking for. Instead, her tension grew ten-fold. She had the unsettling sense her whole life – her very survival, perhaps – hinged on the actions of the next few days. No matter what Mac said or believed, she wasn't ready. Not by a long shot.

*****

It took only three hours to get to the fortress that housed *Luna Ascesa*. Travel in the *Strata* was a much easier proposition than travel on Earth, as long as the traveler knew the journey, rather than the destination, was what mattered. Meg's enthrallment with the *Strata*, and the journey, sped their progress considerably. Mac grinned, wondering how Meg would react to that knowledge.

As he braked the Matchless and cut the engine, Mac heard a tiny gasp escape the woman behind him and turned to look at her. His own breath halted in his lungs and his heart ricocheted against his ribs as he drank in the awed wonder on Meg's face.

A small smile tugged at his lips as tenderness squeezed his chest. There wasn't a doubt in his mind Meg saw his world as a childhood fantasy come to life. She probably saw the flag-festooned cluster of marble, gold, alabaster, and silver buildings with their carved moonstone-pillared passages, as the most and beautiful sight in the world.

He swallowed hard as he watched her, his desire stirred by her beauty, which was so much more than skin-deep. Nothing in all the *Strata* could compare to Meg. His gut clenched in panic at the thought that, in three days, he'd have to give her the choice of walking away. He didn't want to. He'd give up his title, his magic, and even his world, if that's what it took to keep Meg. He realized, with a pang, none of those things mattered without the woman who sat behind him, her slim arms hugging his waist.

He devoured the sight of her, and it was both everything he wanted and not nearly enough. Meg's beauty, which had shown through even the world-weary shell she wore when he first met her, was beyond breathtaking. She was an ethereal entity, as awe-inspiring as the elusive Sylvan Folk, and yet as earthy and solid as the *Thorolfkin*. Without a doubt, he had to find a way to claim her heart.

The need he'd held banked ever since she'd left his bed two nights ago roared to life, unstoppable. Mac bit back a groan and faced forward as he set his jaw against either attacking her with his need or humiliating himself. Now wasn't the time, and this *really* wasn't the place. And, for the first time in his life, he didn't care. Rules and propriety be damned, he needed to convince himself his silence hadn't cost him the most important person in his life. His desire wasn't a simple physical force that could be willed away. This emotion writhed inside of his soul with the need to claim her beyond all doubt, to forever leave his mark on her, before she drifted out of his life. He had to hold her, now, before he did as law demanded and let her go.

As he resolutely slid from the motorcycle and turned to lift her off, Meg regarded him in wary curiosity. Apparently, whatever she saw in his eyes unnerved her, because her beautiful amber eyes darted quickly away, to follow the progress of the small groups of people filtering into the magnificent alabaster building that was the main Hall.

"Do you think we should follow —? Mac, what on earth are you doing?" Meg cut herself off with a gasp as he tugged her gently into the shadows between the oak grove and one of the buildings.

He drew her into the deepest shadows, watching her honey-brown eyes widen in question. With a reassuring smile, he waved a shroud of darkness only a dim corridor of sunlight could pierce around them. He needed her, and he couldn't let her walk into this place with anger still hanging between them, but he wasn't about to put her on display for the world either.

"Mac, what —?" Meg's indignation turned to a whimper of desire as he pulled her tight against his body and let her feel what she did to him.

"Forgive me." He couldn't help the note of desperation in his voice. They had no future if she couldn't forgive him, and Mac wanted that future with everything in him. He had to make her understand somehow.

Meg's brow furrowed in confusion. "For what?"

"For not telling you about this, about *Luna Ascesa*," he murmured, having to fight to concentrate on anything but the sight of her lush lips, or the feel of her warm body against his. "For putting you in this position."

A small, wry smile flickered at her lips, and her eyes sparkled as she shifted against him. "I kind of like this position."

"Not what I mean," he managed, his coherence shredding with every brush of her body.

"Mac?"

He met her eyes, saw the heat there, and his heart nearly hammered its way free of his chest. "Aye?"

"Are we done talking?" Her voice dipped to a breathy whisper as her pupils dilated.

"Meg, I—"

"Shut up and kiss me," she ordered, her arms wrapped around his neck as she urged him toward her.

With a muttered oath that made her loose one of those throaty laughs he adored, Mac gave up on coherent thought or speech, and let his body talk for him in a kiss meant to claim her and offer himself as a willing sacrifice.

Her taste was as wild and free as the wood, at odds with the sweet, vanilla scent of her. In anyone else, that contrast might have made him uneasy, in Meg, it only enchanted him more. He craved her on an elemental level, and the reality he accepted thundered in his veins. He loved her, and he wasn't about to let her get away, not unless she left by her own choice. And he would give her that choice, just as soon as *Luna Ascesa* was over and her apprenticeship dissolved. Until then, all he could do was show her how much he loved her. He intended to do just that.

*****

Meg closed her eyes as she let Mac's familiar scent – that elusive, shadowy spice she still couldn't identify as anything beyond "Mac" – and kiss sweep her away, even as her mind catalogued changes to this man she knew so well. Mac was different lately. His lovemaking was more...*everything*.

Not that he'd ever been all about his own gratification, he was by far the most intuitive and amazing lover she'd ever had. He'd always been intense and, until recently, mysterious. But lately, he wasn't just intense, he made love as if he was trying to leave his mark on her. She wasn't about to admit to him he already had.

Instead, she bit her lip against making any noise that might give them away and swallowed back her gasp of pleasure as Mac's hands stroked her breasts through the thin silk of her dress. His head dipped, and his tongue danced along the edge of the sweetheart neckline, then dipped beneath to send heat dancing through her.

"Mac, stop," she begged against his ear, even as her body sought more of his touch. "Someone might see us."

"No, they won't, *m'gradh*," he whispered, his light stubble rasping against her sensitive flesh until she wanted to scream with need. "Your pleasure is for my eyes only."

Meg's eyes opened in surprise at the harsh quality of his statement, and the possessive light in his bronze eyes sent a tiny thrill through her she didn't want to study too closely. She was independent Meg Tempest, who was okay with her disastrous relationship record because she didn't need a man to feel complete. Wasn't she?

Confusion danced through her head, only to be washed away in the riptide as Mac's hands skimmed her body, finding all the places she'd never known to be erogenous before he'd touched them. His large, artistic hands stopped on the soft warmth of her outer thighs, just below the hem of her short dress, and his eyes lifted to hers.

Meg gasped, her heart fluttering madly, at the raw emotion in Mac's eyes. Mac had changed since they'd met at *Hole In the Wall*. That man had been powerful, mysterious and confident to the point of arrogance. True, he still had the power to set her knees – and hormones – trembling with need. And he possessed just enough mystery to keep her mind engaged wondering what he was going to do next. But the arrogance was gone, as if his pride had been wiped away, and his eyes were openly begging, if only she knew what for.

"We need to talk," he rasped, even as his hands edged beneath her skirt and began the torturously slow trek up her inner thighs, setting her insides ablaze.

*Talk?* Meg's heavy eyelids drifted closed as her senses narrowed on the exquisite feel of his fingers nearing the burning apex of her sex. Her legs turned to jelly, and she had to clutch his arms to remain upright. He wanted to talk? *No way.* She couldn't form a coherent sentence around her tongue which was glued to the roof of her mouth as she fought a scream of frustrated need. It was getting hard to concentrate at all, with his fingers tracing those light, sinfully slow circles on her skin. "Mac…"

"After *Luna Ascesa* is over." He moved in closer, pressing her up against the warm, stone wall. "Right now, I want to love you."

Meg's breath stalled completely, and she nodded mutely. She needed his lovemaking like a life-sustaining drug, he was all that made her feel alive and whole. Her breath rushed back on a surprised inhalation as Mac dropped to his knees, his hands skimming her hem up to her waist, exposing her sex to his view. She heard his indrawn breath, and a low oath rumbled from him to brush hot air over her sensitive flesh. Meg bit back a low moan.

"Great Shadows, you're exquisite." His words, full of genuine awe and masculine appreciation, warmed Meg from the inside, and her nipples tightened as her body throbbed with desire. She wanted him. Now. As if he sensed her feelings, Mac's head lifted, and he met her eyes. A small smile quirked on his lips, setting her insides fluttering, until she wanted to beg him to take her.

He leaned forward then, and touched his tongue lightly to the very edge of her sex where the sensitive folds met. Meg jumped with a gasp of surprise as restless need turned to red-hot demand. Her sex throbbed insistently, and her thighs quaked with the need to feel his body there, his hard length filling that clenching ache.

"Mac…" She was begging now, and she didn't care. With one touch of his tongue, he'd shoved her beyond reality and the danger she knew lurked out there. She was safe, Mac controlled this space, and he'd let nothing harm her. Meg gasped as she felt a familiar trembling in her belly. She was so close, now… "Mac, please. I need—"

"Shh." His warm breath fluttered against her throbbing, wet skin and sent erotic shivers through her. Meg felt the tremble grow closer until she couldn't hold back her moan. Her legs grew weak, and she felt like she'd stepped on a madly rocking boat. This was crazy. He'd barely touched her! Her eyes closed, and the sensation heightened until her head tipped back and she loosed a small cry as he slid one clever finger ever-so-slowly between her folds, slicking her heat with her own desire.

She clutched his shoulders for dear life

unable to keep grip of reality as her knees quaked with every gentle stroke of his finger. She was ready to explode, and yet she craved more of his touch – as if it was a lifeline.

Mac delved deeper, his finger feathering over her throbbing clit, and the thin tether of her control broke. Her head thrown back and her lower lip clenched between her teeth, she quaked in the riptide of sensation that pulled her under and away, her world darkening as Mac's name was ripped from her in an involuntary cry.

When she finally drifted back, she could hear Mac's rumbling murmur, the Gaelic rolling over her in a knee-buckling wave as his voice, rough with need and whisper-soft with awe, tugged at something deep inside of her. His finger was still moving softly, drawing out deepening shivers that delved clear to the source of her soul. She opened her eyes, and stared down into his hunger-hot eyes, and gasped as that digit suddenly penetrated her body, rubbing against climax-swollen flesh. Her nipples beaded tighter, and her hips bucked as hot desperation clawed through her. She wanted to scream with raw lust.

The touch of Mac's tongue delving into her wet heat broke a cry from her throat that nearly shocked Meg with its wildness. She didn't know the woman she was in Mac's arms. She didn't know this sensual, carnal creature she became when he touched her. But she liked it. God, did she ever like it! She moaned his name and bucked her hips as he plunged a second finger into her, and a delicious friction began. She could feel a second climax edging in around her…

"Come for me." Mac's hoarse whisper, full of raw want, spiked through her. "Set the wild woman loose for me, *m'gradh.*"

Those words, in Mac's intimate brogue, catapulted her into the cosmos with cataclysmic force. She wanted to scream in protest as his fingers suddenly withdrew, until she heard his low oath and felt her feet leave the ground as the hard, hot length of his erection plunged into her. Their joining was a tremor that shook her world, and her legs locked around his waist as he drove in again and again, even as his hands freed her breasts to his mouth's desperate exploration.

And then, with a jolt, Meg felt reality shatter completely in an orgasmic wave so deep she swore she was dying, even as she heard Mac's husky shout as he gave in to his own release. Meg clung to him, her eyes closed against tears as she faced the truth – she didn't want to leave him. But she would. Because there were some rules she couldn't break.

## CHAPTER SIXTEEN

"Welcome to *Domus Lumus*."

Meg offered a half-hearted smile to the dark-haired girl who was apparently spokesperson for the small group gathered around her. She'd chosen this corner to hide – from her own aching heart as much as the whispers she'd heard on her arrival a short while ago. She wondered if any of these girls could see how much watching Mac walk away from the building's gated archway – without a backward glance – had killed her.

"Hi," she managed in a murmur, hoping they'd go away.

"You're new this year," one of the other girls, a blond, observed. "Bouda, you have to introduce everyone!"

The dark-haired girl smiled in fond exasperation. "Keep your bells on, Ena. I was just about to." Turning to Meg, she shrugged in apology and rolled her eyes. "Sisters."

Meg looked between the two, perplexed. They didn't share a single trait. How could they be sisters?

The redhead just behind the blond laughed, the sound like a cascade of tiny bells. "Oh, none of us are sisters by blood! We're all students from Dalamor, sent by Headmistress Ravensfall to help with *Luna Ascesa*. We're sworn-sisters," she explained, displaying the inch-long cut on her palm. "Not birth sisters."

"I'm Boudiccea Dougal," the dark-haired

girl said with a welcoming smile. "That," she gestured to the bell-bedecked blond who'd spoken earlier, "is Rowena Wahrbaum. The other blond is Heila Freysdotter, and she," she indicated the redhead, "is our resident mind-reader, Deirdre McArslan."

"Meg Tempest," Meg responded quietly.

Deirdre's deep blue eyes widened. "See? I *told* you it was her!"

"Because she has a similar name?" Heila scoffed. "You always were a romantic, Dee."

"She *does* look a lot like Erinyes," Boudiccea said thoughtfully, tapping her chin with one slim, well-manicured digit.

Meg blinked, nonplussed. "*Excuse* me?"

Deirdre stared at her for a long moment, and then blushed, muttering, "We should go, girls. I was wrong."

The rest of the small group gave her odd looks, but followed her lead away. All except the blond, Rowena. She plopped herself onto one of the lavish divans and closed her eyes as if in meditation, an impish smile curving on her Elfin features. Long moments passed, and Meg sensed an awkward tension growing. Was she expected to say something?

Suddenly, Rowena's eyes popped open, their pearly opaqueness fixed directly on Meg.

"She's lying, you know. Dee's *never* wrong." She sat up, setting her myriad of necklaces, bangles, and beaded braids chiming again. "So, *are* you here with Erinyes?"

Meg blinked. "Erinyes?"

Rowena nodded, her bells and silver

chiming again and her eyes lit with excitement. "What's it like, being apprenticed to an *Illuminata*? I've never even met one, before!"

Meg blinked again. "Are you an apprentice?"

"I was, before I went to Dalamor," Rowena confirmed with a smile. "Mistress Tava Seelelesener, the Elven *Skald*, was my teacher. But *Skald* are everywhere, *Illuminata* aren't. What's Erinyes like?"

Meg offered her a wan smile. "I'm afraid I don't even know who Erinyes is. I'm here with Mac… uh, Alasdair MacCorran."

Rowena's pearly eyes widened. "*You're* the apprentice everyone's had a bee in their bonnet about, this year?"

Meg shifted uncomfortably. "I guess."

She winced as Rowena continued to watch her silently. She had no idea why anyone would be talking about her. What had Mac's girlfriend from the pond told these people?

Rowena shook her head. "You don't look like a *Draoidh*, Meg."

Meg cleared her throat nervously. Rowena had no idea how right she was. "I'm still learning."

"Amazing. And you really don't know who Erinyes is?"

Meg closed her eyes and heaped curses on Mac's head for not warning her about the rumors, or telling her anything about this Erinyes Rowena kept on about. She shrugged awkwardly. "I'm afraid not. I'm new to this world, and—"

"But you're the very image of Blessed Erinyes!" Rowena clapped her hands in glee, her laughter ringing like bells. "Oh, what a marvelous tale this will make! I can't wait to get back to Dalamor!"

Meg figured she looked like a lizard, she was blinking so much. She couldn't help it, she felt woefully out of her depth. "Dalamor?"

Rowena's grin widened. "Dalamor Bardic Academy. It's for apprentices of the Bardic Crafts, no matter the tradition, sex, or race. We all become Journeymen, and take advanced classes in lore, storycraft, and Weaver's Magic. At the end of our training period, we're given the choice of either becoming a House Weaver or a Sojourner. House Weavers keep the lore of a particular House, and defend the House with Weaver Magic. Sojourners are rovers. They have license to collect stories and spells, and practice anywhere. They owe no *Aes Historia* – no Tale Fealty." Her eyes danced excitedly. "I'm training to be a Sojourner. The Sojourners are permitted keys to the gates of the *Tempus Strata.*"

Meg smiled politely, without a clue as to what Rowena was talking about, but liking the outspoken young woman with her bold dreams.

Mac was right, she decided as she listened to Rowena talk about Dalamor, and the Bardic Arts. His world was unlike anything she'd ever encountered. As best she could determine, this world was a collection of dimensions and planes, joined by a single network of interlinking portals and tunnels. The people she'd met so far possessed awesome powers, but also a naïve kind of innocence that had long since been lost in her own world. That naiveté was disconcerting to a woman like Meg, whose world was filled with monsters and horrors that wiped away innocence practically at the cradle.

"Isn't there ever any danger around here, or is this some kind of Garden of Eden?" The words flew from her mouth before she realized what she was saying, and Meg's eyes widened in horror at her own rudeness.

Rowena stared at her, her pearly eyes wary. "Garden of Eden?"

Meg blushed, recalling these people weren't immersed in the same biblical culture she was. "Paradise."

Rowena smiled in understanding. "I've heard tales of the *Terra Strata*. They say it's a place of equal measures of joy and fear. I heard a creation tale, once. It said that, in the beginning, a common bond joined all the *Strata*, and anyone could travel freely over them. Then the *Contra-Magi* and the *Tötenmensch* came, and they caused such destruction in the name of fear that Terra was closed off from the *Strata* for many centuries. Only with the coming of the new generations, who have learned to harness magic on their own, has the *Strata* been reopened to those deemed worthy of the trust, and capable of dealing with the—" Rowena stopped suddenly, jerking from her tale so fast her bells and beads made a discordant clatter. "We aren't supposed to speak of them. Only Masters are permitted, if the need arises."

"Of who?" Meg's brow furrowed. Mac hadn't told her there was any danger or any subjects considered taboo. Her heart thudded dully. Just how bad was the danger?

Rowena glanced around, as if to be sure no one else was listening, and leaned forward to whisper, "The *Saguis Domini*. They are an evil people, consumed by their quest for power. It's said they use the blood of their victims to foretell their futures and placate their evil Deity."

As she listened to Rowena, Meg felt a chill crawl along her spine. Rowena was genuinely terrified of the mere idea of these people. She couldn't blame the other woman. She'd felt that kind of power-hungry bloodlust aimed at her before. If only she could remember where, or when.

*****

Mac sank onto one of the plush benches that lined the atrium of the *Domus Magisteri* and closed his eyes in a combination of weariness and concern. He hated leaving Meg the way he had, but he knew the truth, and he refused to lie to himself. He knew, had he looked back, he would never have been able to leave her at all. Even now, an uneasy impatience ate at him. Meg needed him, his senses screamed, though his brain was hard-pressed to come up with the reason why.

"Well, well! So you made it after all!" Geoff's exuberant greeting boomed in the atrium like a cannon's blast as his large hand clapped Mac's shoulder.

Mac cracked one eyelid and shot his friend a wry look. "Aye, and now the whole *Strata* knows."

Geoff's head cocked to one side, and his gaze grew watchful. "You look beat, Mac. Long trip?"

"In some ways. It's been a hellish month, Geoff."

The blond giant cast a swift look around as he dropped into one of the padded chairs. "Really? So, young Ms. Tempest gave you problems, did she?"

Mac bit off a sharp laugh. Problems? Hell, yeah, she'd given him problems, starting with the sexual tension she stirred merely by breathing and including the near disasters and broken laws that came from trying to train her.

"You could say that, Geoff," he agreed, lowering his voice until he was sure only his friend could hear him. "You set me up to train an *Illuminata*, you know."

Geoff's azure eyes widened in surprise. "You're kidding! She's *Illuminata*?"

"I wish I was joking," Mac muttered, and shook his head as his thoughts drifted again to Meg, and his gut clenched in a familiar tug of worry and need combined. "She has the eyes and the birthmark."

Geoff whistled beneath his breath. "Amazing."

"That's one way to put it."

"Hey, wait a minute." Geoff suddenly sat forward, his eyes narrowed. "The *Illuminata* marks are supposed to be in hard-to-see areas. How do *you* know she has one?"

"I saw it." Mac closed his eyes as the memory of that night slid through him. He'd done more than look, he'd touched it – with his lips. But he wasn't about to share that piece of information. Some things, even thirty years of friendship didn't make acceptable. If Geoff knew Mac at all, he probably already knew he'd crossed the line.

"I see." Geoff's tone confirmed Mac's suspicions.

"Screw you." Mac scowled at his friend. "The mark's on the back of her *neck*."

"Uh-huh. And, as I recall, the lady in question has long hair. Not to mention you're bristling like a *Thorolfkind* guarding his territory." A smug smile pulled at the blond giant's lips, but his blue eyes remained worried. "Do you know what you're doing, Mac?"

That question brought every instant of the past month flooding back. Every precious memory from the moment he'd first looked down into Meg's honey-brown eyes, flashing with anger, to the look of rapture on her face as she came apart in his arms a short while ago. His chest tightened with a tender ache that made breathing hurt.

"Aye," he answered his friend in a gravelly whisper. "I'm in love with her, Geoff."

\*\*\*\*\*

In the shadows of a pillar, Valentina

Crawford clenched her hands into shaking fists as she listened to the two men talk. There was no way she was going to give up her chance to make the MacCorran name, and its prestige, hers. Alasdair had to choose her. She'd leave him no choice.

## CHAPTER SEVENTEEN

There was someone in his room. Even as he closed the door to the shadow-draped domicile, Mac sensed the invisible presence. He drew in a breath, and the shadow-scent he caught was at once familiar and unknown. His heart sped up and his gut tightened as he realized his intruder was female. The only woman who would have reason to believe she was welcome in his bedroom as Meg. Only, she didn't smell, or feel, like Meg. His brow furrowed. Had she already learned to disguise her scent and presence? Mac grinned. He wouldn't put it past her, Meg was more capable than she realized.

He didn't care how she'd made it here undetected, Mac decided as his cock swelled in anticipation. She was here, and he wanted her to stay. With a flick of his hand, he locked the door and set the wards necessary for total privacy in this gathering of varied powers and abilities. He wasn't about to take any chances Meg might be discovered. She was innocent to the rules they were breaking.

"*Leannan*, why are you here?" He asked softly as he moved toward the shadowy figure sitting upright on her heels in the middle of his bed.

"Where else should I be, but by your side, darling?" The voice that reached him was sultry, seductive, and far too familiar. Mac's desire crashed instantly.

"Valentina!"

"Who else?" Came the purring response that set his teeth on edge with disgust and disappointment.

Fury poured through Mac, and he waved all the room's lights on with a harsh "*Leusair!*"

The lights flashed on, and Mac scowled in disgust at her smug, ruby-tinted smile as she rose smoothly to her knees. In all fairness, Valentina was considered a beautiful woman by many – he'd once thought so himself. But Meg taught him what real beauty was, and it was as much internal as external, and that made Valentina ugly.

She met his gaze, her lavender eyes hot with lust and purpose as she purred, "What's wrong, lover? You look tense. I can—"

"Leave. *Now*." He barked the words with a swift, angry gesture toward the door, releasing the wards and locks simultaneously. "You don't belong here."

"You don't mean that," she pouted prettily, her lips pursed as she climbed from the bed with calculated grace, meant to make her nipples more prominent beneath her thin gown. He bit his tongue to keep from giving her the harsh truth. She did nothing for him because she wasn't Meg.

"Quit posturing," he snapped, instead. "I don't want you, Valentina. When are you going to accept that?"

She stilled, and her eyes narrowed in kindling anger. "You used to. What changed?"

He barked out a laugh. She couldn't be this

thick, could she?  "You ceased to be beautiful or giving and turned into a conniving bitch, instead."

She snapped ramrod straight, glaring at him.  "How *dare* you!  I am Valentina Crawford—"

"And I couldn't care less if you were Blessed Gaia.  You still wouldn't belong here. Now, get out."

She hissed, her eyes sunk to slits of fury.

"It's that little apprentice of yours, isn't it?" She demanded, anger hissing in every word. "Does she let you sample *all* her talents?  She should, with what you're giving her in payment. I bet she gives you all sorts of personal demonstrations…"

Mac's fraying anger snapped at that.  It was one thing to insult him, and quite another to attack the woman he loved with ungrounded insinuations.  He grabbed Valentina tightly by the upper arm and yanked her to the door. There, thrusting open the door, he shoved her through the opening with enough force she stumbled.

"A little advice, Mistress.  Learn to control your tongue, before someone controls it for you," he growled darkly.

She rubbed her arm and glared back.  Mac realized he'd probably bruised her, but he couldn't make himself care.  Valentina couldn't hurt him.  But, as he closed the door, her parting words reached his fury-hazed brain, and his blood turned to ice.

"You'll pay for what you've done, Alasdair.

When I'm done with you, you'll be begging for mercy and the life of that stupid little playtoy of yours."

Mac stood with the door closed, his hand on the knob, and told himself Valentina couldn't possibly carry out that threat. She couldn't hurt Meg. His mind played over the possibilities and found reasons to discard them. She couldn't actually attempt to harm or kill Meg physically, not without risking being Marked for her actions, and Valentina wouldn't risk marring her own physical beauty. Nor could she convince anyone else to harm Meg, for the same reason. And Valentina didn't have a clue how the *Sgàil Ealdhainean* worked, so she couldn't sabotage Meg's performance. That left only one avenue open to Valentina.

Mac's hand clenched on the knob as he fought to draw breath around a sudden wave of fear. Valentina, as a woman, didn't need a *Rectus Alloquium* to approach the *Illuminata*. She could approach freely, with any grievance she felt worthy of their intercession. While Mac didn't honestly believe the *Illuminata* would harm one of their own for breaking a rule that harmed no one, he wasn't willing to bet Meg's life on that. He had to find her before Valentina had a chance to speak to the council. He had to find Meg *tonight*.

*****

Meg hummed to herself as she crossed the pillared courtyard between the main Hall and

dormitories of the *Domus Lumus*. Peace
settled over her with the cool blanket of
starlight, and she smiled. She felt safe, and
whole, here. As if a part of her had come home.
She was at loss to explain the feeling. She
expected to feel out of place, and awkward,
amongst all these people who'd grown up
surrounded by magic. But she felt—

Meg froze as a sensation brushed the edge
of her awareness. Like a breeze, it was gone
before she could identify the source. With a
shrug, Meg catalogued it as an oddity of this
world and continued on her way. She'd taken
barely a handful of steps when the sensation
returned, stronger this time.

Her heart beat hard and fast in her ears as
familiar fear returned, and she swore she could
hear the breath sawing in and out of her lungs
as she quickened her pace, the night no longer
either peaceful or friendly. There was
something out there, in the shadows of the
courtyard. She could *feel* it.

She nearly screamed when a hand
suddenly snaked out of a pillar's shadow and
caught her by the arm. But she sealed her lips
over the sound, calling on her anger. Meg
Tempest was no shrieking little pansy. She was
a woman familiar with her own world, and
knowledgeable of the monsters that lurked in
the shadows. She'd taken lessons in self-defense
as soon as she'd gotten her first apartment.
Instinct sent her free hand lashing out as she
twisted to break free. A large, strong hand
subdued her strike, and she was pulled back

into the shadows, her back impacting a hard chest as her attacker's hand left her shoulder to clamp over her mouth. A familiar voice hissed, "Don't."

"Mac!" She spun to glare at him as he released her. He had a lot of explaining to do! "Were you *trying* to give me heart failure?"

"No." He glanced around warily. "I don't have much time, I'm not supposed to be here."

She blinked at him in confusion as he drew her into the shadows of the columned walkway. "What do you mean? I thought—"

"Masters and apprentices are forbidden contact after nightfall here. It's a rule meant to prevent competition tampering."

A slow smile tugged at her lips. He'd broken the rules for her? A warm feeling spread through Meg, despite her promise to not fall for Mac's smooth confidence. "I must be corrupting you."

She met his gaze then, and all thoughts of keeping things light fled at the hunger that burned like liquid copper in his eyes. Instantly, the thread of resistance snapped, and her body began to thrum with need. Her eyelids felt weighted, even as her lower body burned for his touch. How did he do it? One look and she couldn't wait any longer.

"Mac," she pleaded in a whisper, her breathing growing ragged in her own ears.

He made that purring groan, low in his throat, that drove her crazy, and his hands grasped her hips and pressed her against his body as he backed her against the smooth, cool surface of the moonstone pillar. Her knees trembled and her lower body was heavy and drenched with desire as his erection twitched and hardened against her belly. He swooped in like a bird of prey, and devoured the sensitive expanse of her throat. Dimly, it registered he was branding her, marking her as his alone. She couldn't find the strength to deny him, or even protest. Instead, she pressed closer, her fingers tangling in his wild, dark hair as she urged him on with a moan.

"Please," she pleaded in a whisper as her skin burned everywhere he touched. *Please take me. Please want me. Please love me.* But she couldn't voice any of those desires, so she rocked her hips against the restraint of his hands, bringing their bodies into intimate contact.

Mac's grip changed, and his hands slid down over the undersides of her bare thighs as he lifted her legs around him and ground against her until Meg wanted to scream. She was ready to come, but she craved the feel of him inside her, filling all the emptiness. Pushing him a little away, she moved to the closure of his leather pants, tearing at the unfamiliar fastenings until she freed him to her touch and slid her hands over hot flesh that was hard as steel and smooth as silk. Heat shot through her, and an electric shiver pulsed in her womb. She squeezed lightly and felt him buck into her touch as he groaned her name.

"Take me, Mac."

A guttural growl rumbled through him,

and he shoved the skirt of her dress aside with an impatient yank. The draught of night chill passed over her heated flesh, and she moaned with pleasure as the cold touched her wet, exposed core. Then, in one hot, hard thrust, Mac joined their bodies and the force of that joining jarred Meg upward along the smooth stone. She wrapped her legs tightly around Mac's waist and bit down on a cry of ecstasy as her flesh spasmed with the wonderful ache of fullness.

Mac's mouth covered hers in a deep, hungry kiss, before he drew away enough to murmur, "We must be quiet, *m'gradh*."

The raspy quality of his voice and the hot want in his eyes sent a tiny tremor through Meg's belly. She managed a nod and closed her eyes as she fought to maintain control. She swallowed back a moaning cry as Mac rocked against her, driving himself in deeper. God, she loved the feel of Mac buried deep inside her.

"Meg." Breathed against her ear in that harsh, needy tone, Mac's words sounded like a plea as he whispered, "You have to be careful, *m'gradh*."

His hands slid over her skin like satin and slipped beneath her top to cup her aching breasts. Meg bit her lip against the soft cry of pleasure his touch stirred. His words seeped through her and concern stirred within Meg. Forcing her heavy-lidded eyes open, she saw the mingled want, tenderness, and fear in his eyes.

"Careful of what?" She murmured breathlessly, and then gasped and arched as his thumbs    feathered    over    her    nipples, distracting her.

"Valentina Crawford." His words were a guttural sound somewhere between rage and desire, as she shifted. He was close to the edge, they both were. She could tip them both over with a single move. But she didn't. The anger in his voice told her she should recognize the name he'd uttered. She tried to clear her mind, and remember, but it was a useless endeavor, with her body so on fire.

"Why?"

His dark head dipped to the breasts he lifted in those olive-toned hands, and his breath rolled over the swollen tips as he whispered, "Because she means to harm you, *m'calman*."

With that, he drew her right nipple into the hot cavern of his mouth, even as he drove hard into her, and Meg's world flew apart with a cry she couldn't have contained if she'd tried. Through the rush of blood in her ears, she heard Mac's harsh voice against her ear, whispering her name as her release tumbled him over the edge as well.

Even after the night returned and their breathing calmed, Mac held her, her cheek against his warm chest and pounding heart. Meg drew in a breath that smelled of sex and Mac and felt more cherished than ever before in her life. She wanted to ask him what it all meant – the intensity of their mating, the fear in his eyes and voice a he warned her about Valentina, and, most of all, about the tender stroke of his hands now, as if he couldn't bear to let her go.

Meg bit her lip against tears and settled for the safest question.

"Mac?"

He burrowed his face into her neck, nuzzling softly. "Mmm?"

"Why would Valentina hurt me? I don't even *know* her!"

He sighed heavily and gave her neck a kiss before he reluctantly withdrew, his hands gentle as he reordered her clothes before doing the same with his own. It would have been a sweet gesture, she told herself, if he hadn't been using it to stall answering.

"Mac."

His eyes lifted, and she saw the same fear.

"Quit stalling."

A smile quirked at his lips and then died. "Remember that day at the pond?"

Meg nodded, even as a sick feeling accompanied the memory that flitted back. The beautiful, sophisticated woman with the hateful lavender eyes. Mac had called her Valentina. "Oh, God."

He nodded somberly and glanced over his shoulder as voices approached.

"I have to go." He swooped in on her mouth for a last, feverish kiss, before he disappeared into the shadows. His departing words, spoken directly into her mind, left Meg feeling sick with fear. *Be careful, m'gradh.*

As she sensed his departure, Meg sank to the ground with a stifled sob. Mac's last words, as much as the desperation in his lovemaking, told her everything she needed to know. She'd

fallen for him, and he was telling her good-
bye.

# CHAPTER EIGHTEEN

The alabaster-and-moonstone Hall gleamed with soft white light and danced with rainbows flung from the crystals, suspended by magic that hovered as light sources between the thin ceiling and the windowless room. With an indrawn breath, Valentina Crawford made certain her glamour and wards were firmly in place. It wouldn't do to have even one of these twelve women suspect her ploy.

"Valentina Crawford, Daughter of the *Medicus* of Crawford Clan, what brings you before us this day?"

Valentina flickered a glance up, though she kept her head bowed, as the *Illuminata*'s Mistress, Gaia Mercurius, greeted her.

"Blessed Ladies, I throw myself upon your grace and beg your aid in righting a wrong done me." She kept her hands clasped against her breast and her head bowed in demure humiliation, just as her cousin Finnagas had instructed her when he'd given her the glamour potion. He'd told her which of the *Illuminata* would be easy allies, and which to watch closely to be sure they accepted her words. With his patient tutelage, after she'd run to him in her anger and humiliation last night, she would give her finest performance ever. Valentina swallowed her smug grin and kept her eyes lowered lest their sparkle give her away.

"Of what do you speak?" That voice would belong to Erinyes Korenes, fulfilling her duty as Judge. As the Fury of Retribution, it would ultimately fall to Erinyes to decide Alasdair's fate. Finnagas had warned her to tread carefully with Erinyes. The cautious Judge wasn't easily swayed or fooled.

Valentina drew a breath and schooled her voice to sound wavery with pain. "The *Draoidh* Alasdair MacCorran has defiled my trust, and my body, with false promises."

"And why bring this matter before us? Is it not the domain of the kinship councils to settle such disputes?"

"It is my right, as a woman spurned in force, to seek the retribution of the Sisterhood." Valentina lifted her face and let them take in the dramatic, and painful, alterations the glamour potion had made to her appearance. As Finnagas instructed, she spoke nothing that was based in falsehood, but let them draw their own conclusions, instead. While Alasdair had never made her any promises, the act of sex could be construed as a promise. He'd never raised a hand to her in direct violence, but he'd forcibly ejected her from his room last night, leaving a slight bruise on her upper arm. She and Finnagas had merely enhanced that mark with others. And, from the indrawn breaths around her, Valentina could only assume their plan worked. She contained her glee, dropping her eyes again. She'd promised Alasdair he'd pay for scorning her, and she always kept her promises.

Her eyes lifted and met Erinyes'. Sudden uncertainty stalled her heart as those golden-brown eyes narrowed. Erinyes looked familiar, especially wearing that suspicious expression. Did the Judge suspect her duplicity?

"The man who has done this must face Judgment!" Niniane verch Myrrdin, the *Illuminata*'s Purveyor of Rights, cried in outrage.

Frigga Thorsdotter, the Valkyrior, seconded that, adding, "He must be Marked. It is the only fitting punishment for this crime."

Erinyes rose to her feet, silencing the mutters and curses. Her amber gaze passed soberly among her sisters, before she spoke in a clear, commanding tone. "We are not a council made to decide the course of kinship vendetta. Ours is the duty to hear all sides, as brought before us by the Judges of each Clan or House that we may know for ourselves all that has happened."

Heads nodded solemnly, and Valentina' chest tightened as she saw them being swayed by Erinyes' calm logic. This wasn't how it was supposed to be! Panic clutched Valentina.

"He attacked me!" She cried out, heedless of her lie. "Punish him! You're the Fury of Justice! You—"

"Know my place," Erinyes stated firmly, her unwavering gaze on Valentina. "I am the voice of justice, Mistress Crawford, not vengeance."

"My sisters, there is but one course open to us now," the soft, calm voice brought even Erinyes' attention around to the dark, otherworldly gaze of the *Illuminata*'s Oracle, Deborah. Valentina froze. Of them all, Deborah was the most dangerous foe. But if she suspected Valentina was being false, she gave no hint of it as she said, "The *Draoidh* MacCorran must be brought before us, if he doesn't come to us of his own volition, soon."

"Why would a guilty man come to his judgment willingly?" Frigga demanded.

Deborah smiled serenely, even as Gaia rose to her feet. "What is our verdict, sisters? How shall we proceed in this matter?"

Erinyes' eyes narrowed on Valentina again. "Let us send Mistress Crawford with our Healer, Ariel, to determine the extent of the damage inflicted, before we decide what punishment is merited."

Nods of agreement met this suggestion, and Valentina blanched with rage. Were all of these women blind? Why couldn't they take her on her word?

"Blessed Ladies!" She burst out in protest. "There is more to my tale! You have yet to hear the most heinous of his acts."

Erinyes' blond brows drew together. "What is more heinous to a woman than rape or beating?"

"The flaunting of the laws by which we all live," Valentina replied proudly. "MacCorran has defiled even the ancient laws set down by this council's predecessors governing apprenticeship."

"If you speak of the woman he mentors, we already know. Our judgment on the matter was that it is a minor enough matter," Frigga said dismissively. "It defies tradition, not law."

"But he has visited his apprentice's bed," Valentina blurted.

Even Erinyes appeared startled by this news, though Deborah's expression remained unchanged.

"You are certain of this?" Erinyes demanded, her gaze openly angry. Valentina felt triumph swell.

"As certain as I can be without being in the same room."

Erinyes and Deborah exchanged a look, and Deborah nodded slightly. Erinyes turned her stern gaze back to Valentina.

"This matter no longer concerns you. Our judgment on your plea remains unchanged. Please accompany Lady Ariel for examination."

Scowling, Valentina snapped her jaw shut and did as commanded. Just before the door closed, she saw the faint smile on Erinyes' face as she glanced again at Deborah, and had the sinking feeling that she, not Alasdair, would bear the Mark first.

*****

He was worried. Mac had no trouble admitting Valentina's threat made him uneasy. He already knew she was capable of petty, vindictive acts. The only thing that gave him some measure of relief was knowing Valentina possessed no great magical talent. Even as an apprentice, Meg had more power and skill than Valentina would ever possess. However, Valentina's ability as an actress and manipulator worried him.  He couldn't afford to underestimate Valentina's only skills.

Restless, Mac wandered through the conference Hall, exchanging pleasantries where he couldn't escape them, but his focus on finding Meg among the clusters of apprentices. He'd screwed up, last night, he hadn't explained the danger she was in.  He had to make sure she understood.

"She's a *Sgàil Ealdhainean* apprentice?"  A voice near him caught Mac's attention, and he paused.  A glance told him the question had come from someone in a small group of young people wearing the blue-and-gold baldrics of Dalamor Bardic Academy.  A blond, Sylvan girl, two dark-haired girls wearing the colors of Clan MacBandon, and a boy in the pure green of the *Holen Folc*.

"She doesn't look like *Sgàil*," the boy scoffed, and Mac followed his gaze toward the terrace.  His heart caught as his eyes landed on a familiar tumble of dark curls over a scarlet-and-black dress. *Meg*. "She looks like Apollonius."

"Are you kidding?"  The blonde Sylvan shook her head, causing a cascade of beads and bells to chime.  "She looks more like Erinyes."

"Erinyes is blonde."

"True, but wait until she turns around," the girl insisted.  "I tell you, the resemblance is uncanny!"

Mac, unable to tear his eyes away from Meg, frowned as he considered the girl's words. He knew he should move on.  His mother would be appalled.  Moira MacCorran believed eavesdropping to be as great a crime as burglary. Mac couldn't find it in himself to be ashamed right now. This was his only means of knowing what went on with Meg outside of conference or gala. He was too desperate for reassurance she was being cautious to care about propriety. He was too afraid Meg had brushed off his warning.

"Master Jasper says she's the very image of Madame Erinyes," one of the dark-haired girls – obviously twins – agreed readily.

The Sylvan girl shook her head again, setting her bells jingling. "She doesn't even know who Erinyes is. She's from the dimension of the *Contra-Magi*."

Mac froze. While he might have doubted they were talking about Meg before, there was no doubt now. He listened closer, his heart pounding. What did they see that he hadn't?

"Well, that explains it, Rowena," the boy said, with a nod. "They say Erinyes' daughter was spirited away, for her safety, by a nurse from a mortal line."

The Sylvan, Rowena, nodded excitedly. "Say, wasn't that child's name Megara?"

Mac's throat closed as he finally realized why Meg had always seemed so familiar, and why she bore the mark of an *Illuminata* and had no memory of her past. She was a true-blood Daughter of the *Illuminata*, and Erinyes Korenes' long-lost child. Which meant the man who'd tried to abduct the newborn Megara Hermenes was, thanks to *his* bet, finally aware of where Meg was.

Mac's chest tightened painfully at his own stupidity. With his bet, he'd placed Meg in more danger than he'd ever suspected possible. Her life – her very soul – might be in jeopardy. And *he* was the one who set the events in motion. Mac's fists clenched. He'd just have to see to it Meg came to no harm, even if it cost him everything he had.

*****

Meg drew in a deep breath of the cleanest air she'd ever tasted and sighed. She enjoyed the semi-solitude of the outdoor balcony, overlooking a lake that sparkled like clear crystal. It was so beautiful here, and she felt an odd combination of contentment and wariness. Why, she wasn't sure. The contentment, she understood. She felt at home here, these people accepted her without reservation and, though their surprised expressions when they first met her were unsettling, they seemed to neither notice nor care she wasn't like her peers. She'd thought it just a quirk of Mac's, to accept so easily, but she was beginning to see how his world had shaped him to judge a person's soul, rather than their mind or body.

A shaft of longing wound through her at the thought of Mac. She missed him. Her bed felt cold and lonely, and she craved the chance to merely feel his presence beside her, his arms around her. She wanted to tell him of her day and hear about his. To share the quiet and know she wasn't alone in the dark. But, more than anything, she craved the safety he represented. Meg shivered as she felt the crawling sensation that told her she was in danger return – the same sense she'd had since Mac had first mentioned *Luna Ascesa*. As at home and welcome as she felt here, Meg knew she was in danger. She trusted Mac to keep her safe in this world she didn't know.

She glanced up at the slowly rising moon and sighed again. She'd had enough. Mac had taught her to bend shadows so she could make her own dreams come true. Well, being with Mac was more than just a dream. No one said she couldn't use the skills he'd taught her to find him.

Slipping into the shadows, she cloaked herself in one, and moved stealthily from the emptying Hall toward the *Domus Magisteri*. As she made her way through the wooded gardens, the sense she was being followed – which was impossible – pricked her. She nearly jumped out of her skin, and her disguise, as the underbrush near her rustled with movement.

Meg loosed a small scream, her magic abandoned in frightened surprise, as a huge gray wolf sprang from the thicket, straight at her. She dropped to her knees and covered her head with her arms, squeezing her eyes closed as she prayed for deliverance.

"You shouldn't be out here alone, *jente*," a deep voice growled.

Meg lifted her head slowly, to find a giant standing over her, his huge hands planted on leather-clad hips and his azure eyes worried beneath long, wild hair so blond it looked white in the moonlight. She gasped as recognition slapped her. The coffee shop!

"Y-you're Mac's friend," she managed, her voice slightly unsteady. She glanced around warily. "Th-thank you. There was a wolf here—"

"And he still is." He smiled reassuringly as he offered her a hand in rising. "Sorry if I frightened you. It's my experience that *Draoi* who skulk around are up to no good."

Meg blinked, and she felt dizziness assault her as she realized what he was saying. She felt her knees quake and would have crumpled back to the ground if not for his strong arms. "You… you're…"

"Geoffrey Grayson, Master *Skald* of the *Thorolfkin*," he introduced himself jovially. "And you, little Meg, are quite a surprise."

"You're a werewolf!" She finally blurted in surprise and then felt a blush creeping up her neck at her rudeness.

"Watch it, *jente*," he warned. "If you weren't my best friend's lady, I might take offense to that. I'm a *Thorolfkind*, a dark wolf. Not the same thing."

Meg pressed a shaking hand to her forehead. She couldn't think, her head was pounding too hard. "It's not?"

He chuckled. "No. We're both lycanthropes, if that's what you mean. But the Were gain their power solely from the moon and only in the darkness of night. They are a cursed people. *Thorolfkin*, like me, change at will. We are blessed in our ability, and we control it, rather than being controlled by it."

Meg's knees wobbled threateningly again. "I...I think I need to sit."

Geoffrey's keen eyes sharpened as he frowned and led her to a bench carved into one of the huge oaks. "Are you all right?"

She offered him a wavery smile. "I think so. There've just been so many surprises, and I keep feeling like I'm in danger. Having a huge wolf leap at me was just too much, I guess."

His frown deepened. "So where were you sneaking off to then?"

Meg's cheeks heated with chagrin. She was caught now, so she might as well confess. At least Geoffrey claimed to be Mac's friend, maybe he'd understand. "I was trying to find Mac."

A grin split Geoff's face, before he threw his head back and laughed – a great, bellowing howl of mirth. "Mac's got himself a handful, all right! *Jente*, you're lucky I caught you and not one of the other patrollers. There's a good share here looking for an excuse to skin Mac. You don't want to be giving them any ammunition, do you?"

She gasped, and her heart spasmed in fear. She hadn't considered the danger Mac might be in. She honestly had never imagined a man like Mac could ever be in danger. "Oh, God."

Geoffrey was watching her with sympathetic approval. "You really do care about him, don't you?"

She smiled sadly. "I love him."

Geoffrey grinned, draping an arm around

her shoulders companionably. "That's good. Mac's—"

Meg glanced up at a startled oath in a very familiar voice and gasped as her eyes collided with bronze ones dark with betrayal. "Mac!"

As she leapt to her feet, he whirled on his heel and disappeared into the darkness, and Meg felt her heart crumbling around her feet. "Mac…"

Geoff's hand fell on her shoulder. "Leave me to handle this, *jente*. You wait here, I'll send him back to you."

Her chest so tight she could barely draw a breath, Meg could only nod as she sank back to the bench. She felt as if someone had ripped open her soul. What would she do if Mac refused to listen? She closed her eyes and felt the dampness of tears on her cheeks. He had to listen, because if he didn't, nothing would ever matter again.

# CHAPTER NINETEEN

Alasdair MacCorran did not sink to petty displays of temper, Mac reminded himself darkly as he prowled his room in angry circles. But damned if it wouldn't feel good to smash something with his fist– particularly the face of a certain backstabbing friend. Mac bit back a wild yell of rage as the image flashed through his mind again. Geoff, with his arm around Meg and his head bent close to hers. If he hadn't seen it with his own eyes, Mac would never have believed his friend capable of duplicity, or Meg of infidelity.

He closed his eyes, and the memory of Meg's face, the expression of total rapture as she came in his arms, tore across his mind. Did she show that untamed side of herself to anyone else – Geoff, perhaps? Did his friend know what it felt like to—? Mac swore and slammed his fist into the wall until pain washed away everything else. Everything except the hollow ache in his chest.

"I hope that was worth it. Feeling better?"

Mac whirled, scowling at the blond giant who lounged carelessly in his doorway with a blandly curious expression on his face. "Screw you."

"You're not my type," Geoff said easily. "But that raging psychopath display must make you a real hit with the ladies."

Mac glowered. How dare Geoff make light of the whole incident! "Get lost, Grayson.

Now's not a smart time for you to be around me."

"Now's the perfect time," Geoff countered, and uncrossed his arms as he stepped into the room and closed the door. "We need to talk about what you think you saw."

"I *know* what I saw," Mac bit out as he glared at the man he'd called friend.

"That sounds just like the MacCorran I knew – thirty years ago. No one could tell you anything then, either." Geoff shook his blond head with a snort of disgust. "Hela's tits, man, I don't know what Meg sees in you."

Mac's knuckles cracked under the strain of his tendons clenching. "When she could have you, you mean?"

"You blind, pompous *ass*!" Geoff growled, throwing up his hands. "That woman's not interested in me at all!"

"You two were sure cuddling up out there in the garden," Mac shot back, unable to keep his pain and rage out of his voice. "And here I thought you were my friend."

"I *am* your friend, you dumb *uekte*. Though Thor knows why, sometimes!" Geoff met his glare head-on. "And Meg and I weren't 'cuddling.' I scared the shit out of her, an accident, she wasn't very steady. I helped her sit down and was keeping an eye on her stability. It's not every day one of her upbringing comes across a shape-shifter. We were talking about *you*, Mac."

Mac froze, as his protective instincts warred with wary disbelief. "Why'd you scare her?  What was she even doing out there?"

"I was on patrol and thought she was up to no good.  I didn't recognize her scent, and she was in shadow.  She was looking for you."

Relief rushed through Mac, washing away his anger and making him tremble.  Meg had been using what he'd taught her to find *him*.  He felt like a fool, forever doubting his friend's loyalty.  He and Geoff had maintained a long friendship because they had similar beliefs about honor and integrity.  The truth was, *Meg* was the one he was uncertain about.  As much as he wanted to believe she loved him, she'd never given him a single hint she wanted anything more than sex from him.  And that was driving him crazy.

"Where is she?"  He asked his friend quietly, his anger gone.

"Right where you left her, I imagine." Geoff opened the door, and stopped.  He turned then, to pin Mac with a hard, azure gaze. "You hurt her, Mac, and I'll be the first to stand witness for your Marking."

Mac gaped, nonplussed, after his friend as Geoff disappeared through the door.  Whatever they'd discussed, Meg had clearly left an impression on his jaded friend.  And Geoff's meaning couldn't be clearer.  It was time for Mac to do some serious groveling.

*****

Mac stopped in the shadows a short distance from where Meg paced and smiled as he watched her.  Her hands were twisted together and her teeth worried her lower lip in familiar motion that told him she was worried. His heart thumped hard. She was so beautiful and stronger than any woman he'd ever known.

"You'll wear a pit through the world, pacing like that."

She jumped, clearly unaware of his presence until he spoke. Whirling to face him, her eyes filled with an anxious, wary light and, in the moonlight, he could see they were red-rimmed with tears, though her face was dry. Those tears punched Mac in the gut, and he felt his legs tremble. He'd give anything to erase those tears.

"Mac?" Her voice was tiny and whisper soft, as if she wasn't sure she should believe her eyes.

"Meg, *leannan*," he murmured as he strode to her. He didn't stop until he had her securely in his arms, her cheek resting against his chest. "Sweet Shadows, I'm so sorry, Meg."

"I was… I wanted to find you, to be with you," she mumbled against his chest, her fingers digging into his skin as she clutched fistfuls of his shirt. "Geoffrey—"

"Shh." He pressed tender kisses over her face, and his body stirred with familiar desire at the sight and scent of her. He angled her body closer to his as he nipped her ear lightly, dragging a moan from her, and whispered, "Please forgive me."

She nodded mutely, and her tongue darted over her ripe lips as honey-brown wells of want met his steady gaze, and he felt himself sucked into the whirlpool.

With a groan, he lowered his head and took possession of her mouth, drinking in the tiny sound she made as she opened herself to him, her body pressing wantonly closer. His hands slid over her, feeling every tremble of her body through the thin layer of their clothing. But it was the naked hunger of her soul, melding with his, that urged Mac to slow down. He couldn't force or beg her to say words she might not want to say, but he could give her everything he had to give until she couldn't bear to let him go, either.

*****

Meg sensed the change in Mac's kiss even before it disappeared. She moaned in protest, pressing closer when he tried to ease away. "Mac—"

"Shh." He silenced her with a soft, brief kiss so tender it ached in her soul. When he kissed her like that, she could almost believe he loved her. "I want you in a bed."

She opened her eyes to the flames of starlight dancing in his bronze eyes. She tipped her head back and reveled in his embrace as the stars filled her vision.

"Here," she whispered, gripped by a desperation she couldn't name, the need to be a part of both Mac and the nature that surrounded her. "Make love to me here, Mac."

She met his gaze and saw a flare of understanding and hunger, before he stepped far enough away to ease her dress up over her head and off, baring her skin to his hungry gaze. Meg felt the cool air brush her burning skin, her nipples puckered from the combination of cold air and Mac's hot stare.

"Meg, *m'gradh*." His voice was a deep, raspy rumble, the brogue so thick she could barely understand him. Yet, on a level she didn't comprehend, she understood every endearment and promise that rolled from his lips as he stroked and worshipped her body.

She was caught in the fire of the magic Mac created with his touch, she barely felt the bed of soft moss that reached up to cradle her, or heard the symphony of starlight that bathed them both. Mac's touch was all the magic she'd ever need.

Meg arched up with a panting cry as Mac spread her legs and bent to flick his tongue along her hot, wet center. His rumble of appreciation spiked along her nerves, even as his fingers delved lightly inward, spreading wetness and heat in their wake as they opened her to his sight and the cool night breeze.

"So beautiful, so perfect," he murmured, and his eyes locked with hers as he slid one finger down, piercing her body in a sweet thrust. Meg moaned, trying to clamp her thighs closed, to hold him there, but his big body held her spread wantonly open to his pleasure, heightening her arousal. She felt the tension in her lower body growing, even as he chuckled and slowly drew his finger over inner muscles as he withdrew, stroking the spot deep inside that made her arch and purr. "*Milis piseag*. My beautiful *gradh*."

The adoring light in his eyes tripped Meg from reality to pure sensation. She wanted to touch him like he was touching her, flesh on needy flesh. "Mac…"

"Aye, *m'gradh*," he whispered as he bent to blow his breath across her wide-open sex.

"I want to… Mac!" She groaned his name, arching into the sensation of his skilled tongue playing her like a beloved instrument. She couldn't breathe, and the world ebbed in and out on tides of uncontrollable sensation until she couldn't bear it any longer, and she exploded in a shower of starlight.

As she drifted back, she felt the gentle shockwaves of Mac's touch as he continued to stroke her lightly, his fingers on her breasts, her inner thighs and her belly.

"Mac," she whispered, reaching for his shirtfront. "I want to touch you."

He smiled languidly, pressing soft kisses to her throat as he murmured, "You do, *m'gradh*. In ways you don't even know."

"That is so not what I mean," she quipped, offering him a sly smile as she sat up. "Now, lose the shirt."

He laughed but did as she commanded. Meg held her breath, releasing it in a small sound halfway between a sigh and a laugh as she stroked her hands over his hard pecs and abs, drawing a low rumble of pleasure from him.

"What?" He demanded, his gaze intent on her in a way that made Meg's breasts tingle and her womb clench.

"You remind me of a tiger set to pounce, when you do that," she managed with a weak laugh.

His dark brows dipped, and he loosed a growl that danced gooseflesh along her skin before he pounced on her, bearing her back to the ground and skimming his hands over her in a way that made her squeal with laughter. "Mac!"

"I have you at my mercy," he boasted, his head at a rakish angle as he knelt over her.

Meg's lips flickered in a smile. At his mercy? That's what *he* thought. Slowly, she slid one hand up his chest, even as her other dipped to cup against the bulge in his crotch. She heard his intake of breath, saw the shock in his eyes, before he gripped both of her hands and pressed her to the mossy ground.

"What are you playing at, Meg?" He asked in a husky voice.

"No games," she murmured, licking her lips with the need to taste his kiss, his skin. She was on fire, and she needed him to douse the flames, before she exploded. "I just want you. Only you."

The flame in his bronze eyes was breathtaking as he bent to draw her aching nipple into his mouth. He suckled greedily, and Meg twisted against his restraint, desperate to touch him and have him inside of her.

Finally, she worked her hands free and pushed against him until she reversed their positions. Straddling his hips, she felt the bulge of his confined erection against the sensitive juncture of her thighs and nearly purred with pleasure. With a sly smile, she shifted her hips and watched his eyes darken as he hissed out her name. She reached down and undid the fastening of his pants and delved in, releasing him.

Meg sat back on her heels and admired the hard length of his erection, her breath shallow with want. She'd seen a lot of naked bodies as a child, during Marjory and Lee's nudist phase. None came close to the sheer perfection of Mac's sculpted flesh. For a man capable of conjuring anything he needed or wanted, he had the muscular physique of a man who worked hard for everything he had. And speaking of hard…

Meg slid her fingers over his erection, loosing a small moan of delight at the feel of silky skin over hard flesh. Mac drew in a sharp breath of pleasure as his body flexed into her touch. "Meg."

She watched in fascination as a pearl of moisture formed on the tip of his cock, until the swollen, needy feeling became too intense. Straddling his hips again, she sunk herself slowly onto him and felt Mac's strong hands grip her hips. With his hands urging her on, she settled to the hilt on him, a tiny shiver ripping through her at the fullness of him. The world faded away as she rode him, each thrust driving her higher, until the starlight exploded through her, even as Mac stiffened and roared her name. But, as she dropped to the cradling warmth of his arms and chest, Meg had the uneasy feeling they were about to be torn apart forever.

## CHAPTER TWENTY

One more day. Meg blinked blearily as she entered the conference Hall. The full moon would rise to mid-sky tonight, and she would be required to perform the routine Mac had gone over with her before they left Washington. She would have been nervous about that, except the overwhelming sense of dread – the feeling something deadly loomed before her – overshadowed every other emotion. She wanted *Luna Ascesa* over, she wanted as far away from this feeling as she could get. It kept growing, like a shadow looming over her—

"Just who do you think you are?" The hissed voice, high with fury, snapped Meg's attention around to the blond woman whose hand had just clamped with bruising strength around her upper arm.

"I don't know—" Meg stopped, the blood draining from her head with dizzying speed as recognition hit her. *Valentina!*

"That's right, you little whore," Valentina Crawford sneered, her lavender eyes crazed with hate. "You know who I am, and I know who *you* are!"

"What did I ever do to you?" Meg frowned, confused.

Valentina laughed bitterly. "It might not be a crime to sleep with another woman's intended in *your* world, but here, it's a crime punishable by death."

A chill wrapped around Meg's heart, and

she felt her world spin out of balance.  *Oh, God.*  "Intended?"

"Alasdair MacCorran."

A ball of sick dread burned in Meg's stomach, and she closed her eyes against the urge to be ill.  It wasn't true.  Not again.  Not Mac.

"It can't be," she whispered, more to herself than to the furious woman before her.  "He *swore* to me—"

Valentina's answering laugh was mocking. "You deluded little fool!  Men will say anything to get you into bed, don't you know that?  Don't you even know what you are?"

Meg's head spun.  She had no idea what Valentina was getting at but she had a feeling it wasn't good.  "What am I?"

"Oh, this is so rich!"  Valentina crowed, her eyes alight with a malicious glee that sent a shaft of discomfort through Meg.  "Alasdair admitted everything to me, little girl.  How he and Geoff made a bet, as a lark, that Alasdair couldn't use the ruse of teaching magic to seduce someone as trashy as your kind."  Her grin was pure malice. "He laughed over it, over how easy you are, and what a misery it was trying to train you until you gave in.  You, little apprentice, were nothing more than a wager."

Those words hit Meg in the face, bringing stinging tears to her eyes.  It was happening again.  Another man, another lie.  Only, this one cut straight to her soul, because this time, she'd been fool enough to give away her heart in the bargain.

Unable to stand the cruel, hateful expression on Valentina's face any longer, Meg turned and bolted, wrenching free of the other woman's slackened grasp. She was leaving, she had to. And if she never heard another word about magic, or Alasdair MacCorran, it would be too soon.

She ran blindly, tears streaking her face, through the columned walkways that joined the *Domi* to the main Hall. She couldn't stop. Couldn't stop running, or crying, or hurting. In her blind haste, she crashed headlong into something solid and didn't have a chance to register the impact or react before strong, familiar arms closed around her. "Meg! *Leannan*, where are you going? You're crying!"

"Let *go*!" She screeched, yanking away from him as she lashed out. "Go somewhere else and laugh at me! I don't care anymore!"

"Meg, I'd never laugh—" His hands closed around her wrists, but she twisted away, leaving his hands hanging empty as she glared up at him.

"*Don't*. You're a lying, selfish, manipulative son of a bitch!" She slapped him but found her wrist closed in his iron-hard grasp before her blow even landed.

"Have you run mad?" He grated out the words as he dragged her toward the shadows of an alcove. "What is this nonsense?"

"Nonsense?" She spat the word at him in disgust. "You *lied* to me, *Alasdair*. You swore to me that you weren't married—"

"I'm not," he argued in exasperation.

"Or *engaged*, you lying weasel! You promised me I wasn't a bet, and you were laughing at me the whole time! You made a fool out of me, and I," she heaved a furious breath. "I actually fell for it! I loved you!"

He stilled, his face draining of color, as if she'd actually struck him dizzy. His eyes were full of shock, and his grip went slack in surprise as he whispered, "You love me?"

Meg closed her eyes. She wouldn't let him see the truth – that she was still a fool, and he was right. She still loved him. "Loved, Mac. Past tense. I can't love a man who uses me or lies to me. And you weren't ever mine to love."

And, before he could tell her any more lies she was desperate enough to believe, Meg turned and fled into the nearest building. Anywhere would do, as long as it was away from the one man she would ever love and could never have.

The inside of the building was breathtaking, momentarily stalling Meg's pain with awe. Pure white, and made of some kind of stone that glowed as if lit from within, the walls pulsed with a serenity Meg needed badly. Pain came rushing back, and she sank to the floor, her face buried in her hands as she sobbed out all her heartbreak.

"Megara?"

The gentle, tentative query brought Meg's head up, and she gasped, her eyes widening as she stared at the statuesque woman standing over her, worry carved on her patrician features. It was almost like looking in a mirror! The woman was older than her, with faint lines around her eyes and mouth, and her curly hair was a rich, wheat gold. There was sadness in her familiar honey-brown eyes that marked this woman as having lived a long, and not always happy, life. Meg knew exactly how she felt. Her eyes probably looked much the same, right now.

"Yeah?"

"Blessed Kore! It really *is* you!" Suddenly, this dignified woman was on her knees beside Meg, enfolding her in slim, trembling arms as she pressed a kiss to each of Meg's cheeks and then her forehead. "I've heard talk, but when I saw you with Alasdair MacCorran just now, I was afraid the rumor was false. Oh, my darling girl, how did he find you? And why are you crying?"

Humiliation flooded Meg, and she muttered, "It appears I was nothing more than a bet."

One slim, blonde eyebrow rose speculatively. "Really? Well, my darling, I'd say he got more than he wagered on."

Meg blinked, uncomfortably aware this conversation was quickly progressing beyond strange. She was spilling her guts, her most humiliating moments, to a total stranger. And yet, something about this woman made that seem not just safe, but perfectly normal. As if she'd always confided in her. She felt cherished.

"Who *are* you?"

The woman looked startled and saddened. "Don't you know?"

Meg shrugged awkwardly, feeling ashamed for hurting this woman's feelings. "Well, since we look so much alike, I'm guessing we're related somehow."

A smile flickered and spread over the woman's face. "We should look alike. My name is Erinyes Korenes, Megara. I'm your mother."

Meg swore the ground shifted beneath her, or maybe that was just reality warping. She was glad she was already sitting because she was sure she'd hit her limit of shocking revelations for the day. Hell, she'd hit her limit for a *lifetime*.

"My *mother*?" She asked quietly, unable to deny there were similarities between them. At least it would explain why she felt so comfortable here, in this woman's presence. "How? I mean…"

Erinyes smiled gently as she rose and drew Meg to her feet. "Walk with me. There's so much I need to tell you and even more I want to hear."

Meg nodded, her pulse loud in her ears. How many years had she wished desperately for someone to explain how and why she'd been abandoned as she had? How long had she wanted to know who she was, and why she didn't fit in? Erinyes could give her those answers. Meg's heart tripped with anxiety. She was about to learn who she really was and, for the first time, she wasn't sure she was ready for the answer.

As they entered a lush garden at the center of the building, Erinyes smiled at her. "You grew up into a beautiful woman, Megara."

Meg grinned back, in spite of her anxiety. "I think genetics gets more credit for that than me."

"I'm not just talking about the outside, darling girl," Erinyes replied easily. "You are most beautiful on the inside. Your soul is pure and good. Love suits you, my dear."

Bile rose in Meg's throat as her stomach clenched at the memory of what she'd learned about love. "And how does betrayal look?"

Worry furrowed her mother's brow. "Of what betrayal do you speak?"

Meg closed her eyes to hold in the tears that pressed against the backs of her eyes. She really didn't want to reveal the extent of her shame, but this was her mother, and if she couldn't trust that, what did she have left?

"The man I love used me," she admitted in a whisper, her gaze dropping. "He's engaged to another woman."

Erinyes' serene expression struck her as odd, before the woman said, "We shall see. Love seldom leads us wrong, Megara."

Meg cast her an assessing look. What was Erinyes trying to tell her? "What do you mean?"

A gentle smile spread over Erinyes' face, glowing with love and joy. "Many years ago, I too faced the uncertainty of believing I could never have the man I loved."

Curiosity pricked Meg. Could Erinyes' experiences give her the answer to her own painful choices? "What happened?"

"It was the first *Luna Ascesa* I attended after my ascent to the seat of Judge was confirmed. I was destined to a greater cause. But it stung, knowing I might enter that place never knowing a man's touch. I decided I would find a man among the Masters, and go to my duty fulfilled physically, if not spiritually."

Meg sucked in a sharp breath. She could see the danger in that plan. "Did it work?"

Erinyes chuckled. "Not quite as I expected. On the way to the conference, the coach in which I was riding was beset by bandits from the *Saguis Domini*, looking for hostages to gain access to the *Strata*. Realizing they had an *Illuminata* was a bounty for them." She shivered lightly. "I was terrified. Unskilled in the means to protect myself, and innocent to the evils that exist beyond the *Strata*."

She smiled then, her eyes taking on a dreamy quality. "Before they could even lay hand on me, however, *he* was suddenly there. A rogue, dressed in the browns of the forest and draped in a cloak of feathers, his dark hair long and his darker eyes rakish. And I knew he was the one I wanted. My body came alive at the mere touch of his eyes."

Meg smiled tightly, remembering the shimmy in her belly the first time she'd looked into Mac's eyes. Had her body known, even then, what it had taken so long for her heart to learn?

"What happened?"

Erinyes' smile turned wry. "He drove off the bandits, made sure I was all right, and then disappeared back into the trees without even a 'by your leave'."

Meg blinked. "That's *it*?"

Erinyes laughed. "That's what I thought. I was furious. I assumed he was *Magi*, and spent the entire conference searching – pointlessly, I might add – for him. He wasn't there."

"Did you ever see him again?"

"Oh, yes," Erinyes said with a chuckle. "But by the time I did, I was on my way to the ceremony to make me Judge. I was forbidden to consort with any man of magic skill because I could one day be called to Judge him, and a judge must always be impartial."

Meg grimaced. "Sounds like Hell."

"Perhaps," Erinyes conceded with a smile. "It certainly felt like torment to see him again, believing I couldn't have him, ever. I wept, inside, throughout the entire three-day ceremony. When each of the Houses and Clans of which I would be responsible came forward for my *Fides*, I swore I was going to die if I had to see him up close and know which House he was with."

Meg frowned. Every feeling Erinyes described – the knowledge that the only man she craved was forbidden to her – was uncomfortably familiar. The rules she and Mac had faced and finally been forced to break. "You broke the rules."

Erinyes looked surprised but smiled as she shook her head. "No, though it shames me to this day that I was more than prepared to do just that and sacrifice my position and honor. But he never stepped forward with any House or Clan."

Meg blinked, surprised. "So who was he?"

Erinyes' eyes grew soft, and her glowing smile lit her face. "Hermes Apollonius, Headmaster of the Orphian Oracular School. A man totally outside of the jurisdiction of an *Illuminata* Judge, the man who was my destiny and your father."

Meg froze, unable to move as the dreams of a childhood spent wishing for, and dreaming of, a traditional family unit ground to a halt. "My father was… a one-night stand?"

Erinyes' blond brows furrowed in consternation. "I'm not sure what that means, Megara."

"Did you ever see him again, after the night I was conceived?" Meg demanded in frustration. She was beginning to believe all men were lying bastards.

"Of course! As Judge, I'm not permitted dalliances, Megara. We were married a full lunar cycle – a year – before you were conceived."

Meg swallowed hard, shamed by her assumption. Hope sprang to life as she glanced around, wondering if the father she had in reality would do any justice to the one she'd always seen in her dreams. "Is he here?"

"No," Erinyes responded with sincere regret. "Such a pity, too. We were both heartbroken when you were taken away, but we knew Damara would care for you and see you were safe. Still, your father refused to rely on anyone else for that. He maintained his Walks in the Dreamworld, in effort to find you. And here you are, at last, and his wandering soul has taken him off, likely into the wilds." She shook her head in fond exasperation. "He left the same day we arrived, claiming he had a matter to attend to. Oracles."

Even as disappointment touched her, Meg couldn't help but smile. It'd taken her twenty-five years, but she'd finally found the family she'd prayed would make her feel complete. She'd discovered she hadn't been abandoned at all but given up for her safety. She should feel happy and free. So why was there this hollow ache in her chest, where her heart should be?

"Sweeting, you look miserable," her mother murmured, and Meg found herself cradled in the warm arms that had been missing from her disastrous childhood. "What troubles you?"

Meg squeezed her eyes closed, fighting tears. "I feel...*alone*. I shouldn't, but I do. I mean, I'm so happy I finally found you, but..."

"It's not enough," Erinyes whispered knowingly.

Meg sighed, and nodded miserably as she withdrew from her mother's embrace. It felt so natural to confide in this woman she barely knew, as if an impartial counsel listened, and would steer her to the right path, and at the same time love her, no matter her mistakes or choices. She wasn't a freak or burden in this woman's eyes – she was a beloved daughter.

"I love him so much, and I don't really want to believe he's lied to me, but I can't ignore it, either." She swallowed hard. "I don't know what to do."

"Did our actions scar you so badly, sweeting?" Regret and sadness radiated in Erinyes' voice. "Can't you even trust the one you love?"

"But what if he doesn't love me?" Meg barely managed to force the words past her lips. She didn't want to think about the possibility.

"I think," Erinyes said, her expression shrewd, "that you need some time, and space, to see the truth." She laid a comforting hand on Meg's head. "And Megara?"

Meg lifted her gaze, to see joy and love shining in her mother's eyes. "Whatever you decide, your father and I will always love you, and we'll always be here for you."

And, with a smile, Erinyes strode away, leaving Meg to sort out her troubled thoughts and feelings. Which wasn't an easy thing. She wasn't a restful person when she was troubled. Meg's meandering thoughts took her back through the conference gala and out onto the wide, bridged veranda that crossed a gleaming pond and river. With a sigh, she leaned on the rail above the water and stared at her reflection as she admitted she'd been warned about Valentina. Mac had warned her, only Meg couldn't remember what he'd said about Valentina. And the only way to find out was to listen to Mac's side of things. Only, she wasn't ready to face him again, yet. She was still too raw.

"So, *you're* the reason for my brother's long

face and surly attitude, huh?"

Startled from her thoughts, Meg turned to find a girl with moon-pale skin, dark hair, and large golden eyes standing barely a foot away. There was something vaguely familiar about the arrogant tilt of her head and the squared, commanding set of her shoulders, but Meg couldn't place her and wasn't sure she rightly cared. Right now, she just wanted to be left alone.

"I don't know what you mean."

The girl cast her a disgusted look. "Aye, you do."

"Look, not to be rude, m'lady, but I really don't—"

"It's Ysabet," the girl interrupted with a *very* familiar, easy grin as she leaned her arms against the veranda's stone rail beside Meg. Her gold eyes stared blankly over the lake. "Ysabet MacCorran."

Meg froze. Now she knew why she'd recognized this young woman. "MacCorran?"

Ysabet nodded mutely.

"You're Mac's sister!" The realization sent a shaft of joy through her, but it was short-lived, replaced by resentment. "If your brother thinks he can manipulate me by sending you out here—"

"Dair would *kill* me if he knew I was talking to you," Ysabet replied with an unapologetic shrug and an impish grin. "He doesn't believe there's any battle he can't fight."

Wry humor twitched at Meg's lips, and she wondered if Ysabet knew how right she was.

Certainly, Mac would never admit there was anything he couldn't handle, and it didn't surprise her his sister saw that flaw, as well. But did Ysabet know about their battle, or its genesis?

"Does that make me a battle?" She asked ruefully.

"No, but getting to your heart is," Ysabet replied candidly. "That's what Dair wants."

Meg snorted. *Yeah, right.* "I hate to break it to you, Ysabet, but your brother doesn't want anything from me beyond my *performance* and a laugh. I'm a bet, and nothing more."

Ysabet laughed quietly and shook her head. "I don't think so."

"Good for you. But it's true."

Ysabet rolled her eyes. "You're both dense, you know that?"

Meg blinked. "Meaning?"

"Meaning my brother's spent the past hour or so moping around in there," she jerked her thumb toward the Hall, "like a wounded bear. I'd say you're a *lot* more than a bet, Meg."

Meg's eyes narrowed. "How do you know my name?"

Those gold eyes rolled again. "I've been hearing practically nothing else for the last hour. 'Meg' this and 'Meg' that. It was cute for the first ten minutes. Now it's annoying."

Meg's heart leapt, hope flooding her, but she quelled it quickly, Valentina Crawford's vicious words echoing in her head. There was no sense denying the truth.

"He made a bet with Geoffrey Grayson.

They were in the coffee shop where I worked when they made it, and I just happened to be there. He would have taken any woman."

Ysabet frowned, her eyes darkening. "I wouldn't put it past Geoff to bet on an apprenticeship, though I'd say he probably had at least one ulterior motive for it, and I definitely wouldn't put it past Dair to take up the bet. Those two have a long history of betting each other into harmless stunts."

"*Harmless?*"

"The apprenticeship. It doesn't really break any rules, and it's just the kind of shaking things up Geoff lives for, even if Dair doesn't." Her gaze leveled on Meg's. "But I know my brother, Meg. He doesn't break the important rules. And he certainly doesn't wager his heart, ever. Not on a bet. And he's got too much respect for women, he'd never seduce a woman he didn't genuinely want."

Meg snorted, and barely resisted the urge to roll her own eyes. No matter what else he was, Mac wasn't the type to share intimate details of his life with his obviously younger sister.

"Mac tells you about all of his affairs, does he?" She couldn't quite keep the defensive bite from her voice.

Ysabet blushed, but laughed. "You know he doesn't, not like you're thinking. Dair thinks I should remain a virgin and completely ignorant of the act, for the rest of my life. But he does tell me what makes the women he chooses stand out, and I've never heard him say as much about a woman as he has about you. I know my brother's heart, Meg, and it's not hard or callous. You're the first woman I've seen him with in years, and I've never seen him like this before."

"Which only proves how desperate he must have been when he took that bet."

Ysabet scowled. "Who told you that lie, anyway?"

Meg raised a brow at her young companion. "Valentina Crawford. The woman he's supposed to marry."

"Marry Valentina? *Hah*!" Ysabet snorted in distaste. "That really *is* a lie!"

Meg's heart lurched to life. Was it possible? "What do you mean?"

"Valentina is a spiteful, conniving, greedy bitch," Ysabet pronounced succinctly.

"You're saying that she and Mac never…?"

"Unfortunately, they did." Ysabet sighed regretfully. "Dair had a brief affair with her, several years ago. He told me he chose her out of pity, but he couldn't keep it up once he realized what she really was. She was demanding, and she wanted things he didn't want to give. He ended things between them after only a few weeks." Ysabet shrugged. "But Valentina's a Crawford to her marrow, and they're vindictive and grasping. Valentina swore she'd get Dair back, no matter what she had to do. Which makes you a threat, Meg."

"Why?"

"Because you have the one thing Valentina never got."

Meg blinked and, when Ysabet didn't continue, prompted, "That would be?"

Ysabet MacCorran chuckled, shaking her head as she pushed away from the rail. "Dair's heart, of course."

With that, the younger woman headed toward the far end of the veranda, where the kids from Dalamor regaled each other with tales. Meg's gaze went to the Hall entrance, and her heart pounded with the possibilities. Somewhere in there, Mac was waiting... for *her*, to hear Ysabet tell it. But why would Valentina lie about her involvement with Mac, unless there was at least some kernel of truth in it?

Meg frowned, wondering whom to believe. She knew it would come down to a leap of faith, but the least she could do was lay out her suspicions for Mac, and let him tell his side. She didn't know Valentina or Ysabet, so she had no idea which of them might be lying. But Mac, she knew better than she knew herself. She could only hope she'd be able to see through any lies he told.

"You look troubled, my dear."

A prickle crawled along Meg's spine, and she turned to face the man who'd appeared at her side. He was older – probably at least her mother's age, with gray hair that brushed his collar and dark eyes as piercing as a hawk's. He had a classically handsome face with a deep scar across his right cheek. He looked like a rogue. Meg frowned. Something about him was prickling her memory – especially his voice – but she wasn't sure it was a *good* prickle.

"Who're you?" She demanded, surprised at the sharpness of her own tone. She had no cause to be rude to this man. Yet, he put her on edge as surely as Erinyes had set her at ease.

He tilted her a rakish grin that didn't reach his cold eyes. "Why, I'm your father, of course! Don't you recognize me?"

Meg's eyes widened before she sighed. Great. "Should I?"

He chuckled, and Meg contained a shudder at the sound. He didn't *sound* fatherly, but what did she know? Anything was better than Lee. "Mother said you disappeared the first day of *Luna Ascesa*."

"I was preparing a surprise for you." He gripped her hand and tugged lightly. "Come with me."

Uneasiness wound through Meg. She should find Mac – they had unfinished business. If nothing else, she should at least verify that this man really was her father. Erinyes would know – but Meg had little concrete proof that Erinyes was her mother either. Meg sighed. She couldn't just accept Erinyes on faith and not give this man the same benefit of the doubt, could she? With a small nod, she made up her mind and followed him away from the Hall.

## CHAPTER TWENTY-ONE

Mac watched the couples twirling on the dance floor morosely. He didn't feel like dancing. Not anymore. He didn't feel like much of anything. It was almost a relief to be in this state of total numbness. The same state he'd been in since Meg had bolted from him with that accusation and betrayal in her eyes, this morning. At first, he'd been shocked, and then angry and finally hurt. By midday, when he'd still not found her, he'd settled into this sleepwalking state, where he no longer felt alive. What did people of Meg's world call it? Ah, yes… an automation. He'd been operating like a machine.

His eyes shifted to the doors, and he wondered if she'd bother to show up for the performance. Not that it mattered. Everyone had seen her now. They knew she existed, and if she suddenly developed an illness, so be it. But he wanted to talk to her. His search had been unsuccessful, earlier, but he wasn't about to leave things hanging between them. He wasn't about to lose her to a lie.

Mac muttered a disgusted oath under his breath. Ysabet was right! He *was* acting like a wounded animal, skulking in the shadows and searching every face for Meg. Yet, he wasn't interested in acting normal. He felt wounded, so he might as well act it. He felt as if his chest had been laid open and his heart removed. Without Meg, the world lost all color and vibrancy. It merely existed and so did he. He could face that fact now. But he didn't have to like it, damn it!

A swatch of deep, royal blue that reminded him of the dress he'd bought for Meg caught his eye, and his breath, as he realized its occupant was making straight for him. His gaze traveled up along familiar curves that seemed somehow more mature, and his lack of reaction troubled him. Surely, he couldn't be jaded to Meg as well, now. Then, his gaze reached honey-brown eyes capped by a springy mass of blond curls, and he suddenly understood. This wasn't Meg.

His heart sank. Not only wasn't she Meg, but he was in big trouble. The woman striding toward him so purposefully was Erinyes Korenes, the Judge of the Olympians, a member of the *Illuminata*, and Meg's real mother. Seeing her like this, he knew that last part beyond doubt. And it was equally clear she had something important to say. He winced inwardly, and braced for the all-out attack of a Fury.

"Have you seen Megara?"

That question startled Mac. She'd skipped all traditional greeting, and her voice was tinged not with the anger he'd expected but anxiety. She wasn't looking for retribution – she was a worried mother in search of her missing child. A child she had already been torn from once.

"No. I've been looking for her all day, myself." He rubbed his neck, unsure how much it was safe to tell her. "Meg and I...ah... had a disagreement this morning."

Erinyes nodded distractedly. "I saw her outside earlier this afternoon, talking to your sister. But when I finally disposed of my last Judgment, she was gone. I thought perhaps you'd sent her to prepare for tonight. But I don't see her here."

Icy fingers ran along Mac's spine, and his breath turned solid and heavy in his lungs. Sweet Shadows! "Have you spoken with Ysabet?"

Erinyes nodded. "She said she left Meg on the veranda. But no one else has seen her since. She's disappeared, Alasdair."

The panic in Erinyes' eyes slapped Mac with gut-twisting force. How could he have been so stupid? Twenty-five years ago, one of these people had forsaken their *Fides* and tried to abduct Meg as an innocent baby. What had possessed him to leave her all alone here, when the same person could just as easily prey on Meg's vulnerabilities to lead her into a trap? Suddenly, her outburst from that morning made a *lot* more sense, and new dread clenched in Mac.

"I'll find her," he promised Erinyes gruffly as he strode away, his bronze gaze already sweeping the crowd with angry determination. He knew whom to ask, now. He would find Meg, no matter what he had to do, and if the bastards dared harm her, nowhere would be safe for them. They would answer to Mac, and he no longer cared if it got him Marked.

*****

Meg felt her uneasiness grow with every step they took away from the safety of the *Domi*. At first, she'd swallowed her protests, remembering Erinyes' tale of how her father tended to wander away from gatherings. She'd probably got her desire to be alone in nature from him. So she'd gone along, admiring the deep woods and the peaceful glens, in spite of the niggling doubt that told her this wasn't right. But they were nearing the other end of the wood, now, and darkness was setting in. She was supposed to perform tonight. Regardless of what else had, or hadn't, happened between her and Mac, she'd made a bargain with him a month ago, and she had to see it through to the end.

"I have to go back," she said, breaking the strange silence that had engulfed this whole trip. For a man who claimed to be so excited to have her back, he'd spent very little time talking. Odd. She tried again. "I'm supposed to perform, tonight."

"Be silent," he snapped, his voice suddenly harsh.

Meg stopped dead as her vague uneasiness shifted into clarity and alarm. This man was dangerous, and not at all like the man Erinyes had described to her.

*He is evil, Megara.* The voice! It was back in her head. She'd thought it finally gone, she hadn't heard it since she'd finally begun her training with Mac. But it was back now and stronger than ever…and *male*, she realized with a start. She'd always been unable to determine that before. *He means you harm.*

She didn't have to be told twice. She dug her heels in and refused to move.

"Where are we going?" She demanded of the man who held her wrist in what was swiftly becoming a vise-like grasp.

"Nowhere you need concern yourself with." He yanked her along, causing Meg to stumble behind him a step in surprise. "Now come along, like a good little girl."

"Like Hell," she muttered beneath her breath and dug her heels into the soft earth.

*Use the power, Megara. It is your birthright. This world and all it grows are bound to you.* She felt a shift, deep within her, and knew the voice was right. She could feel the pulse of the ground beneath her feet and begged it to hold her fast.

She gasped as spirals of root suddenly shot from the ground to twine about her legs in a grip that was tight but not painful. Even immobilized, she didn't feel threatened by the rising vines – she knew they were protection. This man before her couldn't compel her to go anywhere as long as the roots held her.

"You're not my father!" She accused, anger building in a seething fury within her chest. She couldn't explain why, or where it came from, but a part of her howled with the winds of justice demanding retribution for crimes she didn't fully understand. "Tell me your name."

His answering laugh was dark with

derision. "Oh, no. I don't think so, my lady. I know your place, and your ability, probably even better than you do. I've been watching you since before you were born, and I know what you are, who you are, and what you can do. If I give you my name, I give you control of my fate, my life. Names are power, in your hands. A power I plan to exploit not have used against me." He released her and took a step back planting his feet firmly as he slowly brought his hands together in a steepled pyramid style. "You're coming with me, my dear Megara, whether you want to or not. Hermes' allies can't stop that."

He began chanting in a strange language that plunged clear to Meg's source, and sent her reeling back through time and space, her body and life forgotten as she was pulled under by the memories. How the Paths split and the languages of magic divided.

*She was First Among the Blessed, called Sophia by some, Kismet by others. To her fell the task of guarding the World Gate, maintaining the balance of the worlds that made up the Crossroads, and the lives each housed. The mortals of Earth called her Fate, while the elemental forces of the netherworld referred to her as the Fury. She could not die, and her memory was eternal. But when the World Gate was closed after the Exodus of the Magi, she was pulled to her incarnate forms, to learn of all the peoples over whom she would maintain the balance of life and death. With each incarnation, she learned more about those she protected, and those she defended against, and stepped closer to reuniting the worlds on both sides of the Gates. She would not be deterred by her task.*

Meg snapped back into herself to find the man before her trying to yank her loose from her rooted spot. The incantations he used bounced away from her as if deflected. He used the magic of the *Saguis Domini*, and it held no sway over the elemental forces. Then other words fell from his lips, curses that sent a chill through her. He meant to kill her by draining away her power!

Meg clawed at him, her fingers catching on the uppermost clasp of his robes and tearing it loose, even as the roots shrank away from her feet. Meg tried to scream, but the man's hands closed around her throat.

"You're dead now, girl," he wheezed with rage.

"I don't think so, Finnagas Crawford." The voice – mild and male, and exactly like the one she'd heard in her head all her life – spoke from behind Meg, before a large tree limb suddenly came down between her and her attacker with a sickening crack. He screamed as the force of the blow sent him to his knees.

Meg whirled, prepared for a fight, and froze as the shock of recognition hit her. He'd aged in the years since she'd last seen him in her dreams, but she *knew* this man! He'd been her protector from all the nightmares in her mind as a child. His once-dark hair was heavily threaded with silver, now, and his rugged features were carved even deeper, but it was definitely him. He was even dressed in the same clothes, the brown garments that looked made of moss and the feathered cloak.

He smiled gently as he took her hand and drew her away from the cursing man on the ground. And, as she looked into his face, Meg knew this man was her father, as surely as Erinyes was her mother. Her dark coloring had clearly come from this man.

"He's a Crawford?" She nodded toward the man on the ground. "Why would he want to kidnap me?"

Hermes Apollonius scowled at the other man. "Finnagas is power-hungry." He flicked at glance at Meg. "Now, go. You have a performance to give."

She didn't hesitate to follow his instruction. She did have a promise to keep. But she couldn't resist a final, wary glance over her shoulder, before turning her eyes away. Whatever her father had planned, he clearly didn't want her to witness it. Yet, she trusted him much as she trusted Erinyes. And, deep inside, she knew everything was progressing as it was supposed to. If only she could predict her own life as easily.

Shaking at the memory of her close call, Meg stuffed the clasp she'd taken into the bodice of her dress for safekeeping. All she wanted, right now, was to feel Mac's strong arms around her, his presence wiping away this whole ordeal. Dealing with Finnagas could wait.

# CHAPTER TWENTY-TWO

Mac paced the veranda in wide, anxious circles. He didn't know what to do now. He'd spent the evening searching for Valentina, convinced she'd had a hand in Meg's disappearance. But it appeared Meg wasn't the only one to disappear. No one had seen Valentina since midday.

From inside the Hall, Mac could hear the applause that signaled the exhibition as under way. He couldn't make himself care, though. All he wanted was Meg, alive, unharmed, and in his arms. He couldn't stand being helpless. He just wanted Meg back.

"Mac!"

He whipped around at that familiar voice, his heart pounding harshly. If he'd conjured her through his need, it would kill him. But the warm weight of Meg against his body as she rushed across the wide marble veranda and flung herself into his arms told Mac she was real. Relief made his knees quake as he gathered her close and drew in her unique, wonderful scent.

"Meg, *m'gradh*," he whispered hoarsely, uncaring that his voice rasped with his fear and relief. His body responded to her closeness predictably, but he held it under check. His feelings for Meg weren't based solely on sex. Bending his head, he claimed her mouth in a long, sweet kiss, drinking in her tiny moan of pleasure. His desire turned to groveling need, but he suppressed it ruthlessly. It was more important he know where she'd been, what had happened to her.

Drawing away, he smiled at her small whimper of protest, before his gaze dropped to survey her for physical marks. His eyes stopped on her chest, and his brow furrowed at the unnatural bulge between her breasts.

"What is this?" His fingers skimmed the hard lump through the thin material of her dress, and his eyes met hers inquisitively.

"A little souvenir I picked up from the man who conned me into leaving the conference," Meg said, her chin tilted proudly and her gaze telling him exactly how foolish it would be to attempt to lecture her.

"Let me see," he asked instead, his voice calm and quiet in spite of the anger roiling inside of him. He wondered exactly how she'd been "conned" away. But he really didn't want to know. He didn't want to believe Meg shallow enough to run off for sex.

His fingers slid into the front of her bodice, and he fought to keep his responses impersonal as he retrieved the small metal disc. Gold, he realized, surprise and suspicion tightening in his chest. Very few clans used gold in their crest discs, which was what this was. It told him two things, even before he turned it over to see the crest. Whoever had lured Meg away hadn't expected a struggle, and he'd wanted to hurt Mac, or his family, as well as Meg. There was only one family who wore gold crests he could imagine wanting to harm him. The same clan whom he'd suspected from the first. Mac closed his eyes, his teeth grinding together in rage as his hand fisted tightly around the disc.

Meg cleared her throat nervously. "Mac, I know who he is, and he didn't hurt me. His name is Finnagas—"

"Crawford," he supplied in a gravelly, hate-filled tone.

Dead silence answered him. Mac opened his eyes to find Meg's, full of new wariness, fixed on him. She licked her lips nervously, and then managed, "Do you... know him?"

He snorted. "Too well."

She took a step back. "A friend of yours?"

"Closer to an enemy." He glanced toward the Hall. "We can discuss it later, I'll tell you everything. Right now, I need to know if you feel up to performing. If not, I need to go let the Master of Ceremonies know."

*****

Meg froze at those words, her doubts rushing back, sped along by Valentina's claim. There would never be a better time than now to ask the questions burning in her gut. She drew her courage around herself like a cloak, looked up into his face, and asked, "What am I to you, Mac?"

He blinked, shock registering in his bronze eyes. "What kind of question is that?"

"The important kind. And I'd like the truth, please. No fancy parlor tricks or explanations."

His expression remained bewildered, and he watched her silently, his face a mingling of disbelief and wariness. Meg sighed inwardly. For such an intelligent man, Alasdair MacCorran sure needed a lot spelled out.

"I know about the bet, Mac."

His face went ashen in a way she hadn't seen since Carl had finally worked up the courage to tell her he was gay. That look, she already knew, never boded well. Meg's stomach clenched, and she felt sick. She wasn't sure she could handle this, but it was too late now.

"It's true, isn't it?" She asked in a whisper, her heart breaking with every drop of silence between them. She wanted him to deny it, she already knew. That her wish made her the biggest fool yet, she refused to acknowledge, because she knew if he told her he hadn't, she'd believe him. "You made a bet with Geoffrey that you could train me."

He winced, his normally olive complexion turning sallow, but finally nodded. The sick expression on his face did nothing to alleviate her breaking heart. All it did was piss her off.

"How much?"

His brow furrowed. "Excuse me?"

"You heard me. How much did you bet Geoffrey you could do it? What do you get for winning?"

He had the good grace to at least look miserably contrite as he muttered, "Geoff will get Ysabet into Dalamor."

Meg froze, and her anger turned from

white-hot to ice-cold. "I see."

She started to step around him, but his hand was suddenly there, grasping her upper arm to stop her. "Wait! Meg, I swear to you, I didn't... I mean, I wasn't planning on it being you, or..."

Her fury exploded. "Oh, I see quite well! Even slumming, I wasn't good enough for you until you realized I was *Illuminata*, right? I hope your sister's education was worth your life, *Alasdair*." She yanked from his grasp and continued toward the Hall. Just outside the doors, she stopped, and turned back toward him. "Just one more question."

"Meg..."

"Whose idea was it to tack on the part about sleeping with me?"

*****

Mac reeled back with the force of those words, as physical as a slap. She wasn't serious! She couldn't be. But one look in her granite-hard, amber eyes and set expression told him Megara Tempest had never been more serious – or deadly – in her life. She wanted an answer, and damned if he knew what she was talking about.

"What the hell are you talking about?" He managed in a strangled roar. He didn't give a fig if the whole of *Luna Ascesa* heard him.

"I told you, I know about your bet. I just want to know which one of you tacked on the 'sleep with her' clause."

Blood thundered in Mac's ears – hot, raging blood. That surge drove him forward in an angry pounce, and he closed his hands around her upper arms and dragged her against himself as he grated out, "No one had to bet me to love you, dammit."

"So it was your idea."

"Aye!" He practically shouted the word. "And I tried so damned hard to fight it."

She snorted. "I'll just bet."

The blood drained from his head, leaving him dizzy and off-balance, as her words struck him. Sweet Shadows! "You don't believe me."

One of her shoulders lifted in a negligent half-shrug. "You just admitted it was your idea all along to seduce me."

He blinked. Where had she got that idea? Then, looking into the shadows of her eyes, the truth hit him. Beneath her fury was a very real pain – the pain of insecurity. A smile tugged at his lips as tenderness replaced his anger, and his fingers stroked her arm lightly.

"Sweet, sweet Meg," he murmured softly as he stared into her eyes. "I wasn't the seducer. I didn't intend to touch you from the start. You seduced me with your wit and the flash of lightning in your eyes. You snared me with your beauty, spirit, and courage. It was more of a chore to remind myself I couldn't have you than it's ever been to love you."

She swallowed visibly, her beautiful amber eyes the size of dinner plates and her breathing swift as she stared up at him. "You keep saying that."

"What?" He stroked her cheek lightly, loving the feel of her soft skin.

"How it was easy to love me. Don't you mean *make* love to me?"

The breeze curled a wisp of her curly, dark hair over her cheek. With a soft smile, Mac brushed it aside, and bent to nuzzle the soft flesh he revealed. "That, too. But I meant exactly what I said, Meg."

He heard her small intake of breath, and his heart thundered as he raised his gaze to hers, to find disbelief and hope mingled there.

"You...*love* me?" Her query was a breathless whisper. Again, he admired her courage for asking that question.

Mac brushed his lips lightly over hers. What he wanted was a secluded spot, where he could show Meg exactly how much he loved her. But she had a performance, if she was up to it. There wasn't time for anything else. So, lifting his head, he met her gaze again.

"More than I can say, my beautiful Meg."

Her pupils flared, and he sensed the heightening of her arousal, even as she whispered, "Tell me."

Mac dipped his head and gave her a sweet, tender kiss. It would have been easy to get lost in the sweetness of her taste, even easier to drown in the emotions and sensations she stirred within him. With effort, Mac pulled away and murmured, "I love you, Meg. You have a magic greater than anything I could dream of conjuring. For years, I'd been losing my interest in everything. Nothing held any joy.

Then you came along, with your lightning eyes and magic spirit, and now, I look forward to every day for the sunrise and every night for the starlight. I see your beauty and wonder reflected in them. Meg, I—"

"There you are! Megara, darling, I'm so glad you're back!"

Mac bit back a curse as Erinyes swept from the Hall and embraced her daughter. There was no way he could finish the proposal he'd spent last night convincing himself he could say. He'd be heading for the life of a Marked man for sure, if he did, and then what would he have to offer Meg? Nothing.

"I think they're waiting for you inside, dear," Erinyes continued, oblivious to Mac's frustration. Before he could protest, Erinyes drew Meg away toward the Hall, leaving him with empty arms and the burning certainty Meg was coming into her own. He had nothing left to offer her – nothing except himself. As Meg cast a final smile and a last, heated glance over her shoulder, Mac knew he could do one thing – he could make sure she stayed safe. Meg Tempest had suffered enough. He was making it his mission to see she never suffered again.

*****

Meg glanced over her shoulder as her mother shuffled her toward the competition, and her heart stuttered at the sight of Mac, half-bathed in moonlight, half shrouded in shadow. This man was hers, her tutor, her savior, her lover and her guardsman. And she loved him. Shame hit her, and she berated herself for doubting him, or his feelings, even as a hazy memory slipped through her. He'd warned her about Valentina, and now, she knew why. He'd already known about Valentina's vindictiveness. And maybe more. She recalled the day at the pond, when he'd sent her back to the house while he'd dealt with Valentina. Had the blond woman threatened him?

Meg's hand lifted to her lips, where she could still feel the heat of his kiss. In her heart, love and determination swelled simultaneously, and she realized just how much Mac had risked to teach – and love – her. She would make it count. And later, she would give him back everything he'd given her– including the truth and her heart.

As she mounted the stage set in the middle of the huge Hall, Meg heard the murmur that passed through the crowd and felt the avid gazes trained on her, waiting to judge how worthwhile her training had been. She ignored them all as her gaze sought Mac's across the room. Heat and light rushed through her, casting shadows she could grasp and mold within herself. She closed her eyes, and felt Mac's power and mind brush and combine with hers, and understood they were one and had been for some time. She could do what he did, because he'd given her a measure of his ability.

Her heart tripped, and then calmed as she focused on drawing the shadows nestled deep within her to the surface. Mac was right that men and women practiced the ancient arts differently, but these people were wrong to assume the blending of those differences weakened the integrity of the spells. The combination was strength and could lay open ancient magics that a single sex didn't have the power to use properly.

She heard the gasp that went up from the crowd as she laid open the combination of her power and Mac's like a flower's petals to the sun. She opened her eyes, and Mac's slack-jawed expression, and the look of understanding that slowly crossed his face, were the first things she saw. Green-blue light bathed everything, casting flashes of light and shadow around the Hall. Tilting her head up, she smiled as she saw the shimmering crystalline shape of aqua gates. From the shadow memories at the core of her being, she could pull forth her birthright – the World Gate. With it, she could cross easily between the worlds these people navigated the *Strata* to reach.

With an indrawn breath, Meg focused on lighting the shadowed areas of her soul, and pulling the World Gate back within herself, until the light faded to nothingness, leaving the assembled *Magi* to blink and gape. Meg's gaze went to Mac again, and she saw the small smile that tugged at his lips, even as he offered her a wink.

Her heart bloomed with love as she descended the steps amidst thunderous applause and met Mac halfway to the stage, where he planted a very chaste kiss of congratulations on her cheek. It wasn't enough for her. Devilment danced through Meg, and, before Mac could pull away, she whispered against his ear, "I want you inside me. Now."

She felt his start of surprise, and then the small huff of breath that told her she'd made herself clear. He ushered her through the crowd and out the doors, and Meg barely acknowledged the speculative glances and whispers that followed them. All she was aware of was Mac, and the fire that burned within her, for him alone.

*****

Mac swept Meg into his arms as they neared the *Domus Magisteri*, and ignored her muffled gasp of protest.

"Mac, wait! Someone might see—"

"Let them. By the rules of our deal, you're not my apprentice anymore, Meg. What we do—"

"Can still get you Marked," she argued, pressing her hands against his chest. "Mac, I'm *Illuminata*. My mother is—"

"Erinyes Korenes. I know." He nuzzled her neck and worked his way over the delectable column, breathing in her heady scent. Gods of Shadow, she'd driven him crazy up there. He'd felt her power, and the emotions behind it, and known. She was so sweet, his body stirred with the urgent need to feel her, hot and slick, around him.

Meg gasped and arched in his arms, and he felt the brush of her nipples against his chest as she twisted in his arms. He groaned. Her passion freed, Meg was a force beyond reckoning. And she was his. Tenderness twined through his lust, and he knew, tonight, their joining would be different from ever before, because tonight, he intended to have her *reiteachadh* – her promise to marry him.

At the door to his room, however, honor bade him give her one last chance to change her mind. Drawing a steadying breath, he set Meg on her feet and cupped her face as he met her hungry amber eyes.

"Meg, there're things about being *Illuminata* no one's had a chance to explain to you, things you would have learned naturally, had you grown up among the *Lux Magica*."

She cleared her throat, her gaze impatient. "No more lectures, Mac. I'm not your apprentice, remember?"

"Focus, *m'gradh*," he whispered.

Her eyes narrowed in consideration, and he breathed a sigh that she was apparently finally taking him seriously.

"That means love, or something, doesn't it?" Her question startled him.

"What?"

"Graa*gh*." He winced as she butchered the word. "You've been calling me that since…" She froze. "Since Washington. And it means love, doesn't it?"

"Aye." He stared at her, bewildered. "Meg, that I love you isn't the issue, here…"

She cocked him a long look. "Seems to me it *should* be, since I love you so much it hurts."

Mac, in the process of withdrawing his hands, stopped dead. *"What?"*

She pressed against him, and he couldn't hold back a groan of need as her tight nipples brushed his chest and her warmth cradled the raging hard-on he'd been trying to hide since she'd flown into his arms on the veranda.

"I said, love should be the only issue here," she whispered as she hooked her arms around his neck and rose up on her toes to fuse her mouth to his.

*****

Liquid fire shot through Meg as Mac took the kiss from her control, his tongue moving in a seductive rhythm over her lips and darting into her mouth until she was nearly mindless with need. She was hot and restless, and her nipples tingled with the need to feel his touch. She gasped as his hands cupped her rear, lifting her up against his erection.

Mindless with need, Meg wrapped her legs around his hips, bringing him in more solid contact with the point where her desire flared. She broke their kiss to pant, "Mac, how soon can we get naked?"

He chuckled huskily, his hands kneading her ass as he squeezed her closer.

"That depends," he murmured against her ear, then nipped the lobe. Electricity jolted through her, and she moaned and tilted her head back as his mouth moved to her throat.

"On what?"  She managed breathlessly.

"On what you're wearing under that dress."

The heat of his gaze as it raked over the front of her bodice sent pleasant shocks through Meg's blood, and a sultry smiled curved on her lips.  She leaned forward, her arms around his neck as she whispered, "Absolutely nothing."

The flames in his eyes raged out of control as a low growl worked from his throat.  A laugh, low and sultry, burst from Meg as Mac thrust open the door and swept her inside, her back pinned against the door as he peeled her dress top down over her body.  Then, as if remembering himself, Mac stopped, his forehead resting against hers as he drew in heaving breaths.

"Mac?"

"This isn't how I want it to be," he managed in a hoarse rasp, and she could feel the trembling of hard-held restraint.  "Not like this."

"Mac, it's okay—"

"No, it's not," he interrupted sharply as he released her and stalked away a step.  "Ever since we got here, I haven't treated you with the respect you deserve, Meg.  I've taken, and–"

"Do you hear me complaining?"  She demanded, irritated.  "I wanted you to do that, to act that way.  And I want this."

He regarded her from beneath hooded eyes, his gaze so intense Meg thought she was going to explode.  "And I promised myself I'd love you the way you deserved.  With everything I have to give," he whispered at last, and moved in on her. His lips nuzzled her neck, and Meg arched as another electric jolt passed through her.

"Mac?"

"Aye."

"Are we done talking? I need you." She thrust her body forward, feeling the restless ache building toward explosion inside her. If she didn't have him inside her soon...

*****

Mac silenced Meg's groan with a long, tender kiss as he laid her on the bed. Slowly, he slipped her dress the rest of the way down her arms and off, and then stepped back, his gaze fixed on her breasts. They were perfect – just large enough to fill his hands – with soft, creamy skin and deep, rosy areolas that puckered around her aroused nipples. He drew in a breath to control the tight pain in his groin as his body responded to the delectable feast before him. He'd never tire of looking at her.

"Have I told you how gorgeous you are?" He murmured as he skimmed his fingers over her skin. Her flesh was warm and soft, and he shuddered with need. He wanted in her, but, more than that, he wanted to watch her come undone, to know he affected her as easily as she affected him.

Meg's honey-brown gaze locked with his, and he could read her desire. She licked her lips and her warm hand cupped against his face.

"Mac."

He raised a brow as he skimmed his hands down her body, intent on the feel, sight, and scent of her arousal.

She reached up suddenly, fisted her hands in his shirtfront, and pulled him down. "Shut up."

Her kiss was sweet and hot, and he could feel the light that poured from her rushing over him in drowning waves. Breaking their kiss, he dipped his head to her breasts, feasting on the sweet flesh she offered him as she pushed into his touch. His arousal stirred painfully with each gasping mewl that left her, and the dig of her fingers into his shoulders as she wriggled against him was almost too much.

With a growl just this side of savage, he stripped away the remainder of her clothes, until she lay nude before him, the sweet shadow-scent of arousal potent in the air and her eyes hot and dark with need. Slowly, she lifted herself from her prone position, and Mac swallowed hard at the predatory gleam that flashed in her eyes. His heart was thundering, and he was so hard he was sure he'd explode if she didn't stop looking at him like that.

"I think you're overdressed," she murmured, even as her hands slid up under the front of his shirt, and Mac barely suppressed his groan of need. Her fingers were soft and smooth, and pure heaven as they brushed against him with feather-light touches. Her hands moved up, pushing the shirt in eager motions, even as her lips and tongue found his skin and Mac nearly came at the wicked touch. Love, he decided as he threaded her amazing hair through his fingers, was the greatest magic a man could know. It could do things no other magic in the world could hope to accomplish. It could bring even the most powerful man to his knees.

Mac sucked in a sharp breath of surprise as, his shirt disposed of, Meg's nimble fingers dropped immediately to the fastening of his *briogais*. Before he could utter a protest or warning, she had the pants unfastened and pushed down, his sex in her warm, heavenly grip and his soul in her hands.

He closed his eyes, fighting the explosive force building within him as her clever hands moved over him. Then her hands slid around to cup his ass beneath the *briogais*, before sliding the leather down his legs, her fingertips lightly abrading his skin on the way down.

Just when he was sure he couldn't take any more, her touch suddenly disappeared, sending his eyes flying open. The playful smile on her uptipped face, and the mischievous glint in her amber eyes, was too much. Mac stripped off what was left of his clothing, until he stood over her in his naked glory, his arousal heightened by the appreciation in Meg's eyes.

"Do you trust me?" He asked quietly, brushing his fingers over her cheek. He needed her trust, with what he wanted to do.

She nodded mutely, her gaze fixed on his with a faith that caught his heart and breath at the same time. With infinite tenderness, he lifted her hips and legs, and drew her to the very edge of the bed. One pillow slipped beneath her back and two more beneath her hips put her at an enticing angle. Her hands fell flat against the bed, grasping for purchase on the sheets. Gently, he slid his hands up her lower legs to her knees. Hooking a hand behind each knee, he lifted her bent legs apart, exposing her drenched, sweet core to his view. She loosed a small sound, her hips flexing restlessly, and he cupped her sex lightly, applying just enough pressure to make her moan as her hips surged.

"That's it, *m'gradh*," he whispered eagerly as he slid a finger into her, and spread her own wetness through the glistening folds, his eyes fixed on her face. He craved the sight of Meg coming undone, of knowing he drove her crazy with just his touch. "Let go. Come for me, sweet Meg."

Her moans grew louder and wilder as he stroked her repeatedly, dipping in and out, and tracing every ridge and crevice. Her thighs trembled and her toes curled against the edge of the bed as her fingers dug into the sheets and her pelvis shifted, begging for more. The sight sent a nearly painful twist through his gut, and he knew he was lost. He had to be in her, and now.

Meg arched against his hand hard and, in a rasping cry, demanded, "Now. Dammit, Mac…"

He needed no further urging. Lifting her legs until her ankles rested on his shoulders, he drove himself to the hilt in her quivering flesh, a growl working loose from his throat as she cried out in desperate pleasure.

Their mating was frenzied from there, and Mac knew, in some hazy part of his brain that wasn't consumed by Meg, they'd both been pushed beyond their limits. The violence of their joining was both tender and uncontrolled, and he could feel the building pressure. They moved as if made of one mind and soul, and he knew when and where she craved his touch the most and what would drive her over that final edge. He held back as long as he could, clenching his teeth with the effort as her slick inner muscles squeezed and caressed his driving erection. Then, as she tensed, her entire body quivering, he knew. Reaching between them, bodies still joined, he stroked his finger over her center and sent her catapulting into the shadows of release, as she dragged him over the edge.

Long moments later, when reality finally filtered back and he could pry his eyes open, his heart clenched as he saw the tears on Meg's face. Then, as his gaze fell to her lips, and the radiant, satisfied smile there, he understood. Her tears were from joy, not pain. His legs trembled with weakness, and he slowly withdrew. She made a small sound of protest, and then gave him a sleepy, sated smile as he eased her around on the bed, laid down beside her and covered them both with the blankets. She snuggled against him, and he gathered her into his arms as he murmured, "I love you, Megara."

Her lips brushed sleepily over his chest as her eyes drifted closed. And, as he lay there, watching her sleep, Mac knew what he had to do. The Crawfords had attacked Meg when she was vulnerable and unprepared to defend herself. It was up to Mac to keep her safe– his heart demanded nothing less. Even if it cost him everything he had.

## CHAPTER TWENTY-THREE

Twelve sets of eyes watched him cross the alabaster Hall and, expected or not, Mac couldn't help feeling uneasy. These twelve women had the power to take away his rights, his magic, even his life. But they were also the only ones he could count on to help Meg, and so, he had to chance everything else. There really wasn't a choice. Not anymore.

"Alasdair MacCorran, descendant of the *Cheud Draoidh*, Master *Draoidh* of the *Sgàil Ealdhainean*, why have you entered this chamber of Light, sanctuary of feminine mystery, where men may not tread?" The light, but commanding, tone of Gaia Mercurius' voice rang from every surface of the immaculate chamber. Mac bowed low in proper respect then raised his eyes to the dais where the simply constructed, ornately carved seats of the *Illuminata* were.

"I come under the *Rectus Alloquium*, to implore your aid in protecting an innocent, and righting a wrong done to one of your own."

Glances – some surprised and others knowing – passed amongst the women. Mac caught the reassuring flicker of approval in Erinyes' eyes. It was good to have an ally in the Judge, and even better to have the acceptance of the kin of the woman he intended to marry.

"Of what wrong do you speak?" Madame Luminare, Lady of Scholars, wanted to know.

"Twenty-six     moons     ago,     Finnagas

Crawford was passed over for the *Rectus Alloquium*, on the word of Lady Erinyes."

"This is true," Erinyes confirmed.

"Shortly after, a skilled *Magi* attempted to abduct the newborn daughter of our Blessed Judge."

Gaia's brow rose in surprise. "Are you accusing *Vanurus* Finnagas of this crime?"

"Not accusing," Mac said grimly. "I state a fact. Finnagas Crawford was that abductor."

"On what do you base this 'fact'?" Frigga Thorsdotter demanded.

"On his own confession, Great Lady," Mac returned. "He revealed himself to my apprentice."

"And what cause would he have had to do that?" Madame Luminare wanted to know.

Mac cleared his throat. This was the tricky part – to try and explain how he'd learned of the abduction without revealing his own crime. "Because he tried to abduct her before."

"If you refer to the child Megara, she was saved and is safe," Frigga brushed away his words impatiently.

"That was true, until a year ago," Mac agreed. "But no one was aware, when she was spirited away, that she possessed the *Rectus Portacustos* – the Right of the Keeper. In all these years, no one has known, except for the man who attempted to abduct her, until recently."

A murmur of surprise went through the assemblage, and even Erinyes' eyes widened. The *Rectus Portacustos* was rare, even to a child born of an *Illuminata*. It was the incarnation of the First. Such a right hadn't been claimed in the *Strata* in two centuries.

Mac's eyes skimmed the group and stopped on Deborah. The Oracle looked neither surprised nor concerned by the news. Instead, she appeared relieved, a small smile on her face. As the murmurings continued, Gaia rose to her feet and thumped her ornate wooden and crystal staff in a motion that silenced everyone. Her forest-green eyes fixed on Mac sternly.

"How did you reach this conclusion, Master *Draoidh*?"

This was the test, Mac knew. If he told them how he'd touched Meg, shared her spirit for even an instant, he would be sacrificing everything for a Mark. But if he didn't, they would never believe him, and he would be sacrificing Meg's life. The latter option was unacceptable, which meant he could only speak the truth.

"I've felt it and seen her mark."

Frigga's ice-blue eyes narrowed. "How? Did you touch this child?"

"He loves her."

All eyes snapped toward the gently smiling Deborah and only Erinyes appeared unsurprised by the declaration. Mac swallowed hard. This woman could read his mind, and his heart, she knew his fate better than any other here, and hers would be the decision to give blessing or curse. Slowly, Deborah raised her ancient body from her seat, her dark eyes fixed on Mac with the gentle wisdom of a woman who knew some things, even Fate couldn't thwart.

"Come forward, young man," she said in her whisper-soft voice. "Your love for the woman you knew was forbidden to you has brought you here to face your fate, aware that you sacrifice everything by doing so. There is great courage in your actions. You wish only to bring those who might harm her to justice."

There was no question in her voice, and yet Mac bowed his head and murmured, "Aye."

"Does your courage make you wise, or a fool?"

"Neither, Blessed Lady. Wisdom comes from following the laws, and, Spirits of Light and Shadow preserve me, but I can find no foolishness in love."

Deborah's smile twitched. "And what is it you would ask of us? What will you pay?"

Mac raised his head and met Deborah's ancient eyes boldly. "I will pay any debt that is required of me. But I beg of you, do not let Meg suffer for my crimes. Do not leave her to face this danger unprotected. He's already abducted her once. Should he gain the chance to do so again, I fear he will kill her. I can suffer any punishment, if I know she lives, free and whole."

Deborah's wrinkled hand touched his shoulder lightly, and her words whispered against his ear, for him alone. "There is no crime, no debt in love, except loyalty."

She straightened and turned to the council at large. "I have seen this girl of whom he speaks, in my visions. The events of her life have had purpose, until she came of age to be brought to us. She is a bridge between her adopted realm and this realm of her birth. But her power is great, and dark forces covet that power for their own devices. She has need of a protector, a champion who places her life above his own. We have found this champion, my sisters."

Frigga's eyes narrowed. "A champion must be clear of stain. How does he answer the charge against him?"

Mac froze. "What charge?"

Erinyes met his gaze levelly. "Alasdair MacCorran, you stand accused by Valentina Crawford of forcible violence against her person, and misuse of her trust in false words. What do you say in your defense?"

Red flashed through Mac's vision. Valentina. *Again.* He'd had enough. With great restraint, he managed, "The only violence directed against Mistress Crawford is of her own making, Blessed Ladies. She has made accusations based on pure falsehood."

Erinyes studied him silently for a long moment and then nodded. "I see the truth in your eyes, as I saw secrets within Mistress Crawford's."

Deborah regarded them all with her Sage's eyes. "We must act to ensure the Crawford Clan can never again do harm to one of our charges. Especially not Megara. She faces enough danger."

Erinyes smiled at Mac. "Go, now. You have my blessing to remain at my daughter's side.  We shall deal with Finnagas and Valentina."

With a nod and a bow, Mac turned and strode from the Hall, relief bubbling in him.  He hadn't lost everything and especially not Meg.  And, with *Luna Ascesa* behind them, he could finally offer her forever.

*****

Valentina glanced warily at her cousin, fear gnawing at her.  Why had the *Illuminata* called for them both over her charge against Alasdair?  Had they discovered her ploy and Finnagas' part in it?

As they stepped into the Hall, Erinyes' voice greeted them in the commanding tone of her position as Judge.  "Valentina and Finnagas of the Clan Crawford, step forward."

Finnagas looked gray, Valentina noted with a glance at him.  He never worried.  He always had a plan.  But he was worried now.  Fear launched through her.

"Finnagas Crawford," Erinyes' glare bored into the man, and Valentina wilted in relief.  For the moment, while Erinyes' ire was directed at her cousin, she was spared.  "It has been made known that, twice, you have attempted to abduct a daughter of the *Illuminata*.  As a Master *Vanur*, you are well-aware of your responsibilities, and your *Fides*, and you have violated both using the magical rights granted to you to betray us and your kin."  Her gaze narrowed to fiery slits.  "Have you anything to say in your defense?"

Finnagas drew himself up to his full height and returned Erinyes' glare. Valentina winced. Was he an idiot? No one defied the Judge. "I have done nothing that was of my own making, Madame. If you find fault in what I have done, look to your own House and actions, for my actions are simply a response to those."

Fury sparked in Erinyes' eyes, and Valentina cringed, shifting a step away from Finnagas as the Fury thundered, "You attempted to abduct an innocent babe, and then a vulnerable young woman, and it is my belief you have participated in other deceits, as well. You stink of *Saguis Domini*." Her gaze flickered over the women seated on either side of her. "How do you stand on these charges against Finnagas Crawford, sisters?"

It was a simple vote, made by a display of thumbs-up for innocence, and thumbs-down for guilt. The punishment would be Erinyes' to decide, until a Lady of Fates ascended. Valentina shivered with dread at the verdict as, one by one, thumbs turned down across the dais. Erinyes would offer Finnagas no mercy, once the verdict was in. He had tried to abduct her child, after all.

As the final thumb turned down in a unanimous guilty charge, Erinyes turned her gaze back on Finnagas, and Valentina cringed inwardly, wondering if the Judge would simply disintegrate him on the spot. She looked furious enough.

"It is our decision that you are guilty of the

crimes of which you stand accused. For these crimes, you will pay the ultimate price. From this day forward, you will never again be permitted to practice magic of any kind within the *Strata*. You have disgraced yourself and your clan, and from this day forward, no Crawford will be trusted at their word, and all your kin will be viewed with suspicion. And you, Finnagas Crawford, are banished to the realms of the *Saguis Domini*, to bear forever the Mark of the Damned." Erinyes waved her hand, dismissing Finnagas, and a bright light engulfed him briefly, stripping away even the powers with which he'd been born.

Then Frigga rose and clapped her hands sharply. Through the door marched a troop of women clad in armor and carrying weapons. They immediately surrounded Finnagas, but their attention was on Frigga.

"Take this man from out of sight and cast him into the sealed realm of the *Saguis Domini*." She leveled a finger at Finnagas, and a deep, blood red stain appeared across the left half of his face. Valentina recoiled in horror. The Mark!

Finnagas glared at the council but was wise enough to say nothing as the Valkyries led him from the Hall. Valentina swallowed hard, tasting bile, as the Judge's dark gaze turned to her.

"Valentina Crawford, daughter of a disgraced House, second cousin and once-consort of he who has been banished and unnamed, you stand accused of misrepresenting yourself to this council, and plotting petty vengeance without just cause. As you have already addressed this council with a falsehood, and your Clan is distrusted here, you forfeit your right to speak. On your matter, we have already conferred, and it is our judgment that you share a fate similar to your cousin's."

Valentina felt the floor opening beneath her, leaving her reeling and dizzy. Through the water in her head, she heard Erinyes continue, "However, as Lady Ariel believes your crime to be one not of evil intent, but misguided thought, you will not suffer as harshly. You will be exiled and stripped of your powers and birthrights, but you will be given leave to say your farewells to any who wish to hear them, and to choose the realm of your exile, as long as you never again come in contact with Alasdair MacCorran or his kin."

Valentina collapsed, boneless in a combination of relief and grief. She was an exile, stripped of her magic. And yet, she was not doomed. She couldn't have borne living out her days at risk of the *Saguis Domini*, or bearing that gruesome Mark. Some fates, she realized with a shiver, simply weren't worth risking.

# EPILOGUE

*Luna Ascesa* was two weeks behind them, and the New Year was well under way. Since they'd come back to Washington, Meg sensed there was something odd going on. Mac wasn't himself, to say the least, and no matter how she pressed him, she couldn't get an answer to his brooding stares. She only prayed they didn't mean he was contemplating how to say good-bye.

As she passed the bedroom door, she heard a noise, and her brow furrowed as curiosity struck. It sounded like items being dropped. Why was Mac rearranging the furniture?

Curious, Meg pushed open the door, and froze, her gaze fixed on the bag laying open on Mac's bed, half-full of his belongings. Her mouth worked silently for a moment before, in a disbelieving squeak, she managed, "What are you *doing*?"

His head raised, and he cocked one eyebrow at her before returning his attention to the items he was placing neatly into the bag. "What does it look like I'm doing?"

That was so not the answer she was looking for. Meg swallowed back the sick fear that coiled in her stomach. "It looks like you're packing."

"Good observation." He grinned at her, a teasing light in his eyes only made her feel worse.

"Except we just got home. Where are you going now?"

He stopped and straightened as he turned to face her. "Right verb, wrong noun. *I* am not planning on going anywhere." His hooded gaze slid over her. "Not alone, at any rate."

She blinked. "Who's going with you?"

"You, I hope."

Her heart stuttered as hope blossomed. He was saying he wanted her with him. She offered him a playful smile. "That depends. Where are *we* going?"

He smiled lazily, but she could see the thread of tension in his bronze eyes and knew he was uncertain of his reception. "I'm going back to Lachulan. Meg, *m'gradh*, I want you to come with me. Meet my family, and," he stalked to her, his eyes suddenly intent and hot, "maybe start one of our own."

She swallowed hard as the image of having Mac's children, of building a life with him poured through her like warm honey. "As your mistress?"

"As my *wife*," he corrected, his fingers lifting to skim her cheek. "It's the only way, Meg. Someday, you'll be on the council. The only way we can be together then is if we're already wed. And I don't intend to settle for less. I don't plan on ever letting you go."

She smiled up at him. "Is that a proposal?"

He nodded mutely, his gaze intent. She met that gaze and let him read her joy as she whispered, "Then my answer's 'yes'."

Relief and happiness engulfed his bronze eyes, before he swept her into his arms and fused his mouth to hers.    And, as she drowned in his kiss, Meg clung tightly to him. Her powers were an ocean that threatened to drown her, but Mac was there, her island respite.  The life she was agreeing to was one sure to fulfill every desire in her heart, and that, Meg decided hazily, was a fate too tempting to pass                                       up.

"We're here, Miss Miranda."

Miranda Raennia rolled down the tinted windows of the limousine and studied the beach house. The two-story house, situated on a secluded beach along the Californian coastline, along with a dusting of other homes of similar size, shape and color, settled into the rolling hills near Pismo Beach. Weathered by years of assault from rain, sun and winds, the gray wood of the exterior blended into the night. Upon closer examination, however, this house held one vital difference from that of its neighbors. Black blinds covered every window as if a state of perpetual mourning enveloped the home and its occupants. A mist cloaked the house and its surroundings in a billowy cloud, but Miranda could still see brief glimpses of light escaping at the sides of the shades.

Miranda gave her driver, Charlie, a thumbs-up and he switched off the motor. She scooted to the edge of her seat like a child anxious to join her friends on the playground, and studied the house one more time. Without questioning her life-long caregiver, Jerome Pickering, for details, Miranda knew she'd found the right house. And, if her research was correct, the right man.

Gathering her thick, red hair behind her, she twisted a scrunchy around the mass of waves to keep her curls off her face. She opened the car door and swung her legs to the ground. Jerome, the only soul she would allow to second-guess her actions, questioned her, his British accent growing more precise with his distress.

"Are you quite certain, Miss Miranda? Do you consider this a wise idea? I can't help but wonder what your parents would think."

Sliding onto the rear seat again, Miranda sighed and offered him a comforting smile. The ancient face of her parents' former butler and family servant since before Miranda's birth, creased deeper with concern. How could she not love the old man? His undying loyalty to her parents shifted to her after her parents' deaths twenty-seven years earlier. Throughout the years, he'd become her best friend and confidant, as well as her surrogate parent.

"Jerome, relax, man. I'll be totally fine. I'm going to check things out first. Nothing more."

"But this man's reputation leaves me a bit unsettled, Miss Miranda. Don't forget the locals call him the Night Stalker because of his solitary and unsociable habits. Perhaps we'd best return home and seek other, more agreeable male companionship?"

His eyes twinkled a bit with his recommendation and she hated squashing the gentle man's hopes. "Since when do we worry what name locals give someone? Besides, you know how I like challenges. And Damian LeClare is definitely a challenge."

"Perhaps too much of a challenge?"

Stretching her long frame towards Jerome, she tweaked him on the nose before patting the leathery skin of his cheek. "You worry too much about me and I love you for it. You and Charlie hang tight. I won't be too long, I promise."

Without giving him another opportunity to object, Miranda slipped out of the car and began her trek to the beach. The well-worn path guided her behind the house and down to the ocean, leaving some distance between the deck overlooking the sea and the waves rolling onto the sand. A perfect location to do surveillance before contacting her target.

Five young women, most of them close to Miranda's own twenty-nine years, giggled around a small bonfire. Taking off her shoes, she settled on a piece of driftwood close enough to the group to eavesdrop on their conversation, yet far enough away not to draw attention to herself.

"Hey, Carly, someone better fill you in fast. Has anyone told you about the Night Stalker yet?"

A cute, curly-headed brunette shook her head. "I heard a little from my new landlord, but nothing much."

A voluptuous blonde danced around the fire using a wine bottle as a microphone to lip-synch with the music playing on their CD player. In between song lyrics and sips, she relayed the local legend for the girl's benefit. "Well, then you probably haven't heard the best parts. See, this guy came here a long time ago. My mom remembers him living here and she's really old. Anyway, he lives in that house, but he rarely leaves. And no one has ever seen him during the day."

The chubby girl seated nearest the fire couldn't help but add her two cents to the story. "Yeah, and no one knows for sure what he does for a living either."

The attractive blonde shot her a warning not to interrupt her story. "Anyway…" she dragged out the word to emphasize her annoyance at her chubby friend, "people say he's some eccentric scientist working on a cure for Aids because he gets these deliveries of blood and other medical stuff every month."

Miranda stifled a chuckle, bending her head to act interested in a crab crossing the sand in front of her. How could intelligent people believe such dribble and miss the so-obvious truth?